NEVER AGAIN BOOK II

THE BAIT OF CAIN

R.L. BARKER

Rick Barker
Box 2235, 100 Mile House,
BC V0K 2E0

To my dear wife, Marci, who shares my heart for Israel.

To the memory of those murdered in Israel on October 7, 2023, and all those lost in the ensuing conflict.

PROLOGUE

In "Never Again" we watched New York City Detectives Oliver Braxton and Sam Silverman navigate their way to solving the murder of a prominent Jewish lawyer in early 2024, through the growing hatred of antisemitism and even the staged assassination attempt of the president of the United States, which prompted more hatred against Jews.

Since then, in this story, criminal mastermind David C. Cain is still on the loose; Sam has married his sweetheart, Sandra, and relocated to Minnesota, taking a lateral promotion into a new precinct.

But geopolitical tensions continue to increase across the globe as Israel defends itself against attacks from all sides. Despite the ongoing wars, a decision is pending for Sam and Sandra, a decision that will cost them everything, maybe even their lives.

NEVER AGAIN
BOOK II

THE BAIT OF CAIN

1

Winters in Minneapolis, Minnesota are extreme.
Bitterly cold winds transform people into
woolly mammoths with all their layers of
clothing. The city is built for it though. City
planners designed covered glass walkways and
atriums between downtown buildings to brace
against the harshness of sub-zero temperatures.
But the winter of 2024-25 was extreme in a
whole other way.

Riots.

Never seen in the city before, the
Minneapolis police department was
overwhelmed with officers overrun,
overworked and underpaid, doing their best to
quell crowds of protestors that ran the gamut
from peaceful attempts to make a singular
point, to those bent on turning violent, using
protest signs as batons, clubs and window-
smashers for looting. It was rapidly spreading
across the country in the name of freedom and
justice but using subjugation and injustice as
their means.

The protests?

Detective Sam Silverman was in a state of
shock himself most weekends as the protests
mounted against his people - Israel and the

Jews - and anyone who supported them. Ever since the war in Gaza on the southwestern edge of Israel erupted on October 7, 2023, when Hamas terrorists used the final peaceful Shabbat morning of the 50th anniversary of the Yom Kippur War to launch a slaughter of 1,200 people, mostly Israeli but not all, anti-Israel riots have been taking place in most major cities across the United States and increasing in other countries. And then the apparent assassination attempt on the U.S. president by a Jewish activist in April 2024 put it over the top.

Some pro-Israel rallies also took place, which were generally quiet and peaceful. Still, the violence almost always erupted at the pro-Palestinian rallies as extremists, including blatant swastika-flag-carrying Nazis and those just caught up in the emotion shouted into cameras slogans such as "We're taking over! Death to Jews!" And, "From the River to the Sea! "Sharia law for all!"

"Our god is greater!" in Arabic was also a common declaration.

Sam and his new bride Sandra had moved to Minneapolis from New York, taking a lateral 'promotion' for the lifestyle of a safer city, or so he thought.

He ran his hand through his shortly cropped raven-coloured hair as he looked out over

Hennepin Avenue from his office window - that was one of the perks of the move, a corner office with a view over the city and the famous Target Center Field, and, if he squinted hard enough he could see the Hell's Kitchen restaurant, which he and Sandra enjoyed now and then.

He estimated at least 300 people were walking down the main street banging drums, waving flags and chanting "Free Palestine Forever!" He decided to give it another half hour before leaving the office, and instinctively grabbed his phone to call Sandra.

"Sam?" The voice came with a tap-tap at his door and he spun to see Captain Donald Conner. "Got a moment, Sam?"

"Sure," said the lean detective. "I was just about to leave but... what's up?"

"Well, to be honest, I'm just worried a bit about the state of affairs around here."

"Around the precinct? Around the office? Around the city? Around my desk? What do you mean?"

"Yes, exactly," said Conner, sometimes called C.C. for Captain Conner. "All of the above. Well, not your desk; your desk is fine. Things are getting wild out there and it feels like a focused evil. I just read a headline that said antisemitism in the U.S. is up 500 percent since

October 7 and we're only a year away. The U.N. voted overwhelmingly in favour of welcoming a Palestinian State, meaning to give the Palestinians unprecedented rights for a non-member observer state - 143-9 despite October 7. Are you and Sandra doing okay in all of this?"

"Thanks, Cap'n. I appreciate that. We're okay. It's pretty freaky alright. I thought moving here last fall was a step into more peaceful times. New York was getting more than just a little nuts, but it's nuts here too, probably all over. I don't think we can escape it."

Conner removed his dark-rimmed glasses, which was about the only thing that made him look like he had some book smarts. He could have stepped out of a 1940s superhero comic strip or as some say, a Dick Tracy cartoon, with his cut-from-granite type torso and square jaw. He put the corner of one arm of his glasses in his mouth for a second, then removed it to say: "Well, just be careful out there, Sam. Maybe don't be too quick to point out your ethnicity."

As soon as the words were out of his mouth, Conner knew it was the wrong thing to say.

"Sorry man, that didn't come out right. I didn't mean that, Sam."

Silverman fake-sniffed, smiled, scratched his nose and said, "No worries, Boss. I get it. And I appreciate it. We Silvermans are a proud bunch and it has gotten us into trouble before," he said. "Don't worry, though, we'll be careful and we'll be smart."

Conner nodded and started back out the door, paused, looked back and said, "You'd think that the attacks of Hamas would have resulted in compassion for Jewish people everywhere, not the opposite. Crazy. Have a good night, Sam."

"Thank you, sir. You too."

Sam stood in the quietness of the office for a few minutes and then tapped the phone to call home.

No answer.

Christmas music quietly played in the background as Sandra Silverman idled her way down the aisle of Davidson's Market, her favourite little shopping place.

The supermarket, established in 1978 by Zachariah T. Davidson carried almost everything one could need on any given day, including the kitchen sink - literally. Plumbing supplies were in aisle 13, the last aisle of the store.

It was lovingly called "Zach's" by those in the neighbourhood as it was now operated by Zachariah Jr. and his family - wife, Maria and two teens, Asaph Zachariah (called "Ace" by his basketball buddies) and Shelly, the youngest at 12.

Sandra already had what she was looking for, some tomatoes, along with ground beef for tacos, and coffee - Sam loved his coffee; she loved her peppermint tea - she was just dilly-dallying her way through the aisles looking for any sale bins or baskets as Zach always had some hidden treasures if you looked hard enough.

She realized her phone was vibrating inside her purse. She wasn't good at the whole cell phone thing, never has been. Sam insisted she had one, but she'd just as soon talk to people face to face than on the phone, and she was hopeless at texting.

She stopped in the aisle to find the buzzing. Locating it, she realized she missed a call from her hubby.

Oh well, he'll be home soon and I'll have dinner prepared.

She put the phone away and rounded the corner toward the produce again, looking up at the corner convex mirror bulging outward and toward the front counter.

Three young men in balaclavas were milling around the counter. She stopped.

There was no one else in the store that she knew of. She eased her way back behind the end of the aisle, near the toy squirt guns and superhero action figures, and stood silently holding her breath.

The men started yelling and slamming the counter. She watched in the mirror and realized that if they looked back down the aisle, they would be able to see her. She remained as still as she could and noticed she was trembling inside.

The commotion got louder. One of the men locked the main door, while the second pulled out a large pistol and demanded the till be opened, pointing the gun wildly at Zach, who did his best to cooperate, hands in the air, amidst the obscenities and hate language against Jewish people. The third spray-painted a swastika on the front window.

The spray artist then filled his pack with junk food and anything within reach, and then stuffing what else he could into a larger sports bag.

Sandra tried her best to remember what she could about their descriptions but their faces were covered and they wore simple tracksuits. She tried to guess their height and weight.

She quietly, nervously, slipped her hand into her purse and retrieved her phone.

What's the passcode?! She realized that her mind was in a state of panic. Her trembling had become outright shaking. As she typed in the first three digits, she glanced up in the mirror - *good, they're busy* - she punched in the last two digits and her phone came alive.

She tapped the phone tab, and the icon for SAMMY, and the phone did its thing. As she steadied her hands, the unthinkable happened and the phone leapt out of her fingers like a fish jumping out of water. The clash of the phone on the cream-tiled floor was as loud as a crash of thunder over the seasonal tunes. She froze.

The guy with the gun stayed focused on Zach jamming money from the till into a backpack, but the other two spun around realizing someone else was in the store.

~

Sam was driving. His dashboard screen lit up "SANDY" and he lightly touched the key to answer.

"Hello, my love! I tried to call you. Where are you?"

He waited and furrowed his brow as he bent toward the stereo and listened to make out what was on the other end.

"Sandy? SANDRA?! What's happening?!"

He heard men yelling and then he heard his sweetheart screaming his name, "SAM!"

Her phone had slid under the shelving beside a tall basket of pink flamingos but remained on.

2

Sam jammed on the brakes and pulled over to the side of South Washington Avenue to listen more intently to the call on his car speaker.

He could make out men's voices yelling. Sounded like street punks in his ears. He heard the word, "Jew" and it stung. He could not hear Sandra's voice. Then the hair on his arms stood at attention as he heard her scream out, "Noooo!"

It was the distinct double ding of the front door of Zach's Market that made him slam the car into first gear and punch the powerful V6 engine into motion. He knew exactly where this was happening. He just didn't know what was happening. His mind was leaping off in all directions but he was only about four minutes away. He would make it in less than two. He hit the siren on his 2008 Impala as he peeled back out into the slush-covered street, flipping the emergency flashers toggle to the 'on' position for good measure.

"She has nothing to do with this! Let her go!"

Zach yelled at the three men, one at the door, the second pointing and waving a slimline 9 mm handgun right at his face and the third bringing Sandra up the aisle, her hands pressed behind her back. She was crying and stumbling forward.

Zach started to move toward the side of the counter when the gunman yelled at him to stop, which he did... for a moment. Just as one of the trio pulled open the front door to make their escape with their stolen goods, Zach's son Asaph, returning from basketball practice, sauntered through the back door of the building and entered the store near the dairy in full view of the front counter.

"HEY!" He screamed out and began running full-tilt at the gunman, who in turn pointed the pistol in his direction. Zach moved quickly over the counter and careened into the gunman, whose arm flew to the right just as the gun discharged with a loud clap.

His partner in crime who held Sandra took the brunt of the shot but it was a through-and-through and landed squarely into her side, lodging just above her right hip. She dropped like a proverbial sack of potatoes to the floor, pulling the hoodlum down on top of her, as he screamed out at the fire that had erupted in his side.

The gunman now turned his attention to Zach and managed to fire another round before being hit full-on by the charging teenager. He smashed into the gunman like he was hitting a tackling dummy on the high school football field.

The third ruffian split out the door and zig-zagged down the street in and out of the streetlights. People stopped walking and wondered what was happening, trying to discern if they were in any danger. Inside Zach's, the gunman lost his weapon at that point and scrambled to his feet as did Asaph, who faced off with him. The man turned and fled out the front door, tried lifting his downed partner on the way, but he was too much. He was half crawling toward the door. His friend bolted, leaving him where he lay.

"Ya, you better run!" Asaph yelled as the door ding-tingled once more.

He spun about. Sandra was holding her side and sitting by a can of green beans that had abandoned the shelf.

Zach was not moving.

Sam pulled to a screeching halt in front of the store and burst into the market, gun drawn.

"Sand!" He yelled and rushed to her side.

"I'm alright," she said wincing. "Check on him," she nodded toward Zach.

Asaph stood over his father but was paralyzed by fear of his dad lying motionless on the floor.

Sam reached over and put two fingers on Zach's neck. His face was buried in the tile floor and a pool of blood was forming underneath him.

"He's alive," said Sam.

Asaph breathed a huge sigh of relief and then bent down.

"It's okay, Dad. You're going to be okay. He's going to be okay, right?" He looked at Sam.

"I think so, yes. Yes! Of course, he will," said Sam. Pulling Zach over onto his back, he said to Asaph, "Put your hand here and press as hard as you can. Lean into it as if your life depended on it. His does! He took a shot to the right of his heart; it's serious, but I think he'll be okay."

Sam turned back to Sandra, who was breathing heavily with her eyes closed. He called for an ambulance in the same motion as he moved toward her, using the police radio attached to his belt.

"Hey baby, you okay?"

"Think so. Just hurting a bit. I don't think it went in very far. I can almost feel it."

"Okay, okay. The ambulance is on its way. Hang in there."

He squeezed her hand and drew her head into his chest. "Just rest easy," he said. "You're alright." He may have been talking to himself in some ways.

Asaph, who really had saved the day, said, "I need to go tell Mom and Shelly. They're in the house out back."

Sam said, "Just hang on till the ambulance gets here... keep that pressure on your dad. It won't be long."

Far away from the noise of cities and headlines of violence and crime, David C. Cain sipped cammomile tea on the multi-levelled, flowered terrace of a sprawling beach hotel in Manta, Quito, and watched the sun dip silently into the Pacific Ocean. He imagined the hiss it made as it hit the water.

This was his favourite getaway though he had several such places around the globe, Maui, Barbados, Florida and Quito, Ecuador.

Soaking up the warm evening breeze and listening to the pattern of the waves soothed his soul. At least that's what he would tell his guests. He didn't really have friends as one might describe friends. But he had a lot of guests. Cain was more of a loner and didn't like the pressure of accountability in friendships. He would also joke that he didn't have a soul, which some thought might be more true than he knew.

His cell phone vibrated on the deck table beside him. He glanced over at it as it lit up in the greying dullness of twilight.

"Amarillo?" he muttered out loud looking at the screen display.

Amarillo, Texas meant only one thing - family - and he didn't want to talk to family.

He hadn't spoken with his parents for over 18 months, his younger brother, Jonathan, maybe once or twice, and he couldn't remember the last time he talked with his sister Candy, nor his older brother Pete. He was officially "estranged," in his mind.

He let it go to voicemail.

I'll listen later.

He decided he was hungry and was beginning to think about menu choices in nearby restaurants when the phone buzzed again.

Amarillo.

He decided to pick it up.

3

Special Agent Franklin T. Hanover of the Federal Bureau of Investigation (FBI) paused to catch his breath as he exited the Boeing 737 narrow-body aircraft. The humidity of Panama City smacked him like a slap upside the head and he knew he needed to get out of his standardized grey-on-grey suit and black tie ASAP.

He stepped down the steps onto the tarmac reflecting on the five-hour flight from DC to Panama City where "Mrs. Guerrero" stopped chatting only for the meal and snacks, which he thought were rather decent for airplane food.

Need to talk to the Deputy Director about going first-class next chance I get.

His first priority was to get him and his partner, Special Agent Andrew Jackson (A.J.) Davis to their hotel and get a good night's sleep. Tracking down criminals on someone else's turf was never easy.

Having never been anywhere near South America in his life, Agent Davis took in his surroundings with great interest despite the humidity and the setting of the sun, which made visibility difficult.

For a moment A.J. imagined what it might be like to retire to a place like this with the warm sun and nearby Gulf of Panama including the Galapagos Islands just off the coast - but that dream flitted away as fast as a punctured balloon when Frank, or Terry as he called himself now and then (it was technically Franklin Terrance) spoke about the plans for the morning.

"We'll take the first hotel shuttle out in the morning back here. Our flight's at 7 a.m. and it's just a hop, skip and a jump to Quito," he said.

Davis nodded and said, "Copy that," as they headed into the terminal.

Frank glanced back to see if his partner had the briefcase. He did. It contained the million-dollar bait that would hopefully nail Cain, thought Frank.

AJ caught his glance and lifted the briefcase slightly with a smile. He thought he would ask him about the Frank-Terry thing the first chance he got.

Sandra was resting easy now. She had had a two-hour surgery to remove the slug from her side. The procedure went as smoothly as it could have, according to the surgeon, Dr. Aisha Vaughn, who said the bullet had been embedded just under the skin and was still in the fatty tissue.

"Probably hurt like crazy, but was not deep. She's fortunate that it was a ricochet, or how you call a through and through," she explained. "The initial hit took the brunt."

Sam looked at his wife with great love and compassion, wishing it was him lying there, not her, while at the same time thinking about nailing the three punks that had put her there in the first place. But he knew that would be left to the uniforms. She had an IV in her arm and Dr. Vaughn said she'd be kept overnight at least. She would check on her tomorrow before releasing her.

Sam leaned back and tried to get comfortable in a very uncomfortable chair as he pulled a folded letter from his inside jacket pocket. He could hear the voice of his former boss and mentor Detective Oliver Braxton, and he smiled as he thought of him leaning back on his favourite chair, almost snapping it at one point.

"Dear Sam,
I hope this letter finds you well and settling into your new position in Minnesota. Hard to

believe that you took a softie job like that! But I'm glad you did. NYC is getting crazier all the time. I seriously think the world has gone to hell in a hand-basket like my father used to say. I mean the antisemitism was bad enough when you were here, bro, but it's been over the top these days.

You probably won't believe it, but it actually drove me to attend a church service at that big ol' Presbyterian Church on 14th last weekend!

I didn't know…

Sandra groaned and started to stir and wake. Sam folded the letter and put it back in his pocket. He moved closer to her side and squeezed her hand.

Her eyes blinked open.

"Hey honey, how are you doing?"

"I feel like I was run over by a Toyota truck," she said and closed her eyes again.

"I think you mean a Mack truck but I get it. You just try to get some sleep, sweetheart. You'll be out of here in no time."

"Did you catch them?"

"We caught the one that took the other half of your bullet," he said, trying to be funny. He wasn't.

"Did you?"

"Ya actually. He didn't get very far; his friends just left him and he got as far as the sidewalk. Some friends. That dude's in a different hospital and as soon as he's good to go, he'll face charges."

"How's Zach?"

"Hey, you just try to get some sleep alright? Close those puppies and rest now. Just rest."

Sam didn't have the heart to get into it with her. He wasn't exactly sure how Zach was doing, but last he heard it was not going well. He was still in surgery.

Two floors down and behind automatic blue-striped and pinkish-coloured doors, Zachariah Davidson was under the knife as his wife, Maria, son Asaph and daughter Shelly waited in a nearby waiting room.

Maria paced and Shelly sat on the flat blue leather couch staring at her phone.

Ace, as his friends called him, leaned against the wall staring out the window, and noticed that if he concentrated, he could hear the inner workings of the big white-rimmed clock on the wall behind him. He realized he could see it in the reflection of the window, and tried to read it backwards.

Time ticked ever so slowly, then disappeared as he heard the double doors at the end of the hall click before they opened and two people walked out. It was the doctor and maybe an intern with him.

"Mrs. Davidson?" Dr. Geoff Donnelly asked.

"Yes," Maria said, wavering, with her hands clasped near her chin. "Is my husband going to be ok?"

"He's a strong man, Mrs. Davidson. He'll be fine. He lost a lot of blood but we've replaced that and removed a bullet from just under his shoulder and stitched him up. The bullet missed all the main bits. He'll be very sore for a while, and in here for a few days but he'll be fine."

Maria dropped her hands and then brought them back up to wipe her eyes and thanked the doctor profusely.

Ace and Shelly came in for a group hug as the doctors stepped away and took their leave.

"This is the goodness of G-d, the goodness of Hashem. Thank you, thank you, Toda, Hashem," Maria repeated a few times.

Shelly cried with her mom.

Ace was relieved about his dad, but something else burned inside.

Revenge.

4

Attorney John "Jack" Bannister consumed his ham and cheese *"sammich"* as he called it, outside the E. Barrett Prettyman Courthouse in Washington D.C.

He contemplated the three-sided 24-foot granite monument depicting the freedoms of the United States. It was said to exemplify the Constitution and Declaration of Independence. According to the plaque next to it, the obelisk represents the three branches of government: legislative, judicial and executive and the guarantees offered by the U.S. Constitution and the Bill of Rights.

Jack raised his eyebrows in slight protest as he took another bite and chewed his ham, cheddar cheese and rye bread.

He took a final bite and sipped his decaf coffee with the one cream. He was once addicted to the real thing, easily drinking a couple of pots of coffee a day by himself but realized he should quit for good when every time he missed a cup for about an hour, he'd get a dull headache as a reminder. When the headaches got worse - and more symptoms without the caffeine - he thought *this couldn't be good for me* and decided to quit for good. Decaf became his go-to mojo just for the taste and to have something in his hand at certain times. He said he knew that it was only "hot brown water" but somehow it satisfied him. And now he was off caffeine altogether and quipped that he could "sleep nights and stay calm."

He started up the long steps, took a deep breath at the top, adjusted his blue silk tie, and took a 360 view as reporters talked into television cameras about the case soon to resume.

"Today we will hear the closing arguments and it may be the day David Rabinowitz will be found guilty as charged and face at least 25 years in the State Penitentiary, maybe more..." one reporter told his followers.

Another: "You'll recall almost a year ago, our president was shot by a would-be assassin. Did David Rabinowitz make that fateful shot to take out the leader of the free world? Or was it someone else? Who pulled the trigger on April 24, 2024? The people have a right to know, and they'll be looking for justice today. We'll be following every step of the procedure," she said directly into the camera.

Bannister looked to his left. An African American woman did the same and leaned into the camera as if she knew it personally. She editorialized her take on the alibi of the accused. She was sure he was guilty and she let her watchers know it.

Bannister pursed his lips and strolled toward the courtroom.

His client, David Rabinowitz, waited in a holding cell in the lower regions of the old building down the two flights of tiled stairs. A service elevator could be used but for the most part, sheriffs walked the prisoners up the stairs, and down the wide hall to the courtroom. Sometimes serious offenders wore ankle shackles but even they were still made to take the stairs.

"Let's go," county sheriff Kyle Owen said to his captive. Kyle had been an all-state quarterback at Penn State with a dream of playing for the Minnesota Vikings but blew out his right knee, the knee he planted on to throw, and now he worked for the Minnesota State Department of Corrections. He still carried a bit of a limp but did his job with great pride, knowing that one slip could put many lives in danger. He strapped on his belt every morning, complete with mace, taser, gun and handcuffs with his head held high.

Rabinowitz stood and quietly followed Owen out of the cell and down the hall to the steps. He counted each step as he climbed, thinking today might be his freedom day.

His journey into the vortex of the United States judicial system had been arduous and sometimes bordered on the ridiculous, having been pinned for an assassination attempt on the U.S. President. He had been caught in a political pinball game and was relocated from jail to jail after being taken into custody some seven months ago.

It seemed clear to Bannister that this was a terrible mishandling of justice, but he knew that the proverbial wheels turned very slowly and the process had to be followed regardless if he thought it should've been thrown out long ago. A counter-lawsuit was being considered by him and his client.

The fact was, that Rabinowitz was charged with the attempted murder of the U.S. President and there appeared to be good evidence against him. That evidence needed to be diffused before a jury of his peers.

Today was his 16th appearance before Federal Trial Judge Bryce Lawson and a jury of 16, seven men and five women plus four alternates.

The bailiff unlocked the double doors of the courtroom that allowed entry from the main hallway. He propped one of them open and nodded to Jack, who met the nod with one of his own, stood up and walked into the austere hall.

Designed with aged hardwood throughout, the grand sense was one of justice and the rule of law. Large portraits of the founding fathers looked down on the proceedings from various angles ~ Abraham Lincoln, George Washington, Benjamin Franklin, Thomas Jefferson, John Adams, Alexander Hamilton, and James Madison all kept a silent but stern watch.

Jack walked with confidence wrapped in humility to his table on the left side of the room. He breathed in deeply and clicked open his briefcase. He brought out a notepad and pen and that was all. He had his closing speech prepared, memorized and was ready for the drama.

The large six-panelled door to the left of the imposing and ornate oak bench opened up and Rabinowitz was brought into the room.

Reporters sat up and court artists began sketching immediately.

Sheriff Kyle Owen escorted the prisoner to the defendant's table and released Rabinowitz's handcuffs.

"Thank you, sir," Rabinowitz smiled at Kyle as he rubbed his wrists. The sheriff gave only a slight nod in return and took his post on a side chair of the gallery.

Jack half-stood and shook David's hand as the prisoner took his position. They waited for the rest of the scene to unfold.

Sam and Sandra left the hospital that evening with her in a wheelchair because that was the proper protocol. She was sure she could walk under her own steam but the nurse insisted on wheeling her out.

A homeless man approached Sam for a handout. Sam paused.

"Good evening officer, any loose change for a coffee today?"

"How do you know I'm an officer," Sam asked, genuinely wanting to know.

The man, whose gray-brown beard draped over several layers of sweaters and a winter's vest, smiled a toothless grin and responded.

"I get around. Sometimes I'm downtown near the precinct and I see you come and go. My name is Allan."

"Well, you're very observant, Allan. My name is Sam."

"Good to meet you, Officer Sam. Hey, I've got some good news for you. Spring is coming!"

Allan said that with a laugh as it was a chilly November eve.

Sam laughed as he noticed the nurse positioned Sandra at their car door.

"I've gotta go, Allan. Good to meet you. Here's a few bucks. Get some supper."

"Thank you, dear sir. I owe you one."

Sam waved and nodded and nipped over to help his wife out of the wheelchair and into the car. She resisted a bit saying, "I'm fine" but he helped her still.

Once in the car, she asked what that little encounter was all about.

"Oh, he was just looking for a handout for something to eat. I never noticed him before but he knew I was a cop."

David Cain punched in the area code for Amarillo, Texas, taking a deep breath before he did so. He knew it would mean talking to his mom or dad.

He waited while the phone did its thing.

Amanda Cain answered with her usual, "Mmm Hello."

"Hello, it's David. You called."

"Oh David, yes, it's your father. He had a pretty serious heart attack and fell as a result and banged his head; he's in hospital… I thought you should know in case you wanted to see him."

"How serious is it?"

"I think it's pretty serious, David. They're not letting him out; they think he could have had a stroke too, or something so they're checking all that out. Peter and Candy are on their way and well, Jonathan is already here, as you know. We're praying for a miracle."

David didn't respond to her last comment.

"Well, I'm not sure. I can't just pick up and fly to Texas, Mom."

"Where are you?"

"Far away."

"Oh dear. How are you doing?"

"Listen, Mom, I've got to go. I'll see. I'll let you know."

David hung up the phone and looked out over the beachfront, listening to the waves.

He sighed. *I suppose this could be the end of the old git.*

He decided he would consider flying back to Texas to see him one last time… *I'll look into it tomorrow.*

5

Frank Hanover was up early, showering at about 4:30 a.m. while his partner tried to get in as many winks as he could. A.J. Davis got up at about 5 and lugged his way to the bathroom to embrace the shower.

Hanover told him to hurry as the shuttle left at 5:30. "Move it, man," he said, "The day awaits!"

Davis grunted his acknowledgement and shut the door of the bathroom.

Hanover flipped open his laptop and typed an email.

Greetings from Panama, sir,
Arrived. Heading to Quito this morning. We have good reason to believe Cain is at the Grand Talisman Hotel & Suites. This should be an easy one. I'll keep in touch and let you know how it goes.
Terry

He looked at the signature "Terry" and thought back to Grade 7, the year his parents separated, eventually getting a divorce. His father always called him Terry but his mother always called him "Franklin T." She believed it carried more dignity than "Terry" and that it would go a long way in his life in making him the man she wanted him to be. Dad just said, "Terry's fine." *They even argued about that.*

He could hear Davis singing some song of sorts in the shower as he opened the door to the hotel room and picked up the Panama Express Daily off the floor.

Hotels that provide a daily paper are just plain better hotels.

He unfolded the broadsheet and laid it on the round dining table. The front page headline read: "Jews No Longer Safe in Israel."

He read a few lines and wondered if what he was reading was true.

Stop being alarmists. You media mongers are creating unnecessary hysteria. Jews are safer in Israel than anywhere else. They can defend themselves better in Israel.

The article reported how the West Bank, or what the paper called the Occupied West Bank, was becoming a hotspot and was taking over where Hamas had left off in Gaza. It quoted a former IDF Commander saying, "Here, I sit in my house and I know that the IDF is guarding me with God's help. Please don't ignore the direction of America as it pertains to Jews. It's getting really bad, really fast."

It then went on to say an anti-defamation organization had reported that since the Hamas attack on October 7, there have been 3,031 anti-Semitic incidents in the US alone, the highest figure the organization had ever recorded compared to any previous six-month period.

Davis walked out of the bathroom like a new man.

"Wooya! Now that feels good - I'm alive again!"

"Good morning to you too. There are a few breakfast muffins in the fridge. You can warm them up, or... well, suit yourself."

"Thanks. You all ready to go?"

"Packed and pumped, my friend."

"Breakfast muffins...my favourite. And yes, I've got the briefcase well in hand."

Frank leaned to the right to see the briefcase by the unmade queen bed, within grabbing reach if necessary by one who would be lying atop the bed.

He nodded his approval while Davis grabbed a blueberry muffin and popped it into the microwave.

The two were on the shuttle within 20 minutes and on their way to Quito. There was a short delay at the terminal but other than that, everything was going according to plan.

❖

Jack Bannister sat up straight in his chair and watched his State counterpart walk into the room, followed by three lackeys learning the ropes. They could be called upon to do anything from taking notes to finding witnesses to scaring witnesses away if necessary. Whatever it took to win a case, they were ready to do.

The lead prosecutor was Brandon Chandler, a 6'4" DC man, born and bred, even played one season as a shooting guard for the state champion Revolutionaries before a lower-body injury ended his athletics career and launched his legal life as an attorney. His aim was to get behind the bench one day and being hired by the State Attorney's Office was a good start. He knew he had a long way to go but for now, he was an Assistant District Attorney, and sometimes that meant having to make decisions against his own will and integrity.

He was caught in just such a quandary at the moment, knowing that his job was to complete the prosecution of David Rabinowitz, even though somewhere deep inside his gut, he felt the guy was innocent. There were too many questions and "the shadow of doubt" certainly lingered.

"All rise!" The bailiff sounded out as the door behind the bench wafted open and Judge Bryce Lawson graced the courtroom with his presence.

The Judge was a big man, with a handlebar moustache that would even make General George Custer jealous. And, that's exactly the look the Judge was going for. A long-time history buff of the American western frontier, Judge Lawson collected early American memorabilia such as rifles, arrowheads, pistols and knives, and had a large painting of Custer's last stand in the Black Hills of South Dakota above the mantle in his chambers.

Lawson stroked his mustache with his thumb and forefinger and took his seat while the people waited for him to settle.

"Good day, Ladies and Gentlemen. Thank you. You may be seated," he said in a southern drawl, and the gallery all took their seats.

"This Court has heard submissions from both the Prosecution and the Defence in the State versus David Rabinowitz in the matter of the attempted assassination of the 47th president of these United States. We've been through cross-examinations of 13 witnesses. Today we will hear the final arguments from Mr. Bannister and Mr. Chandler. Mr. Chandler, are you prepared to give your summation at this time?"

"Yes, Your Honor."

"You may proceed."

The Prosecution cronies rose as one as Brandon Chandler unlocked his briefcase, popped it open, pulled out a laptop and studied a few notes quietly, then took a sip of water and approached the jury, who had been waiting patiently.

As his team sat down, pens drawn and legal pads ready, Chandler said, "Members of the jury, the State thanks you for your patience and attention to the details surrounding this case. We have, I believe, successfully argued that David Rabinowitz, a decorated rifleman in his own right in the National Reserves, but also an extreme Zionist activist well known for his lawlessness and misdeeds at various times in his life, had both the motive and the opportunity to take the shot at our fine president on April 24, 2024. For heaven's sake, his fingerprints were found on the rifle! And his fingerprints were at the scene where the shots were fired that day."

Chandler paced back and forth in front of the jury, letting his last words dramatically hang in the air. Bannister eyed the jury and could tell that more than one wearied of Chandler's antics.

"The defence has made a whole lot of hullabaloo about Mr. Rabinowitz's Jewish heritage and made him out to be a scapegoat when in fact," he paused for effect. "When in fact it is that very Jewish heritage that the State feels drove him to the hatred of our fine country and the attempt to take down our leader."

The eyes of the jurors followed Chandler as he slowly walked back to his table and took another sip of water.

He spoke for another 20 minutes going over the case details that had been gone over time and again. He finally brought it to a conclusion.

"Ladies and Gentlemen of the jury, I implore you to think of the ripple effect of your decision today. If you come back finding this man not guilty, you will give free rein to all those of the same extremist worldviews to take their potshots at our politicians whenever they have the opportunity, even at the highest level! However, if you find David Rabinowitz guilty as charged in this matter, you will indeed perform your civic duty in laying out a great deterrent to that same criminal element who would do injury to us, and will further the cause of our allegiance to the Flag of the United States of

America, and to the Republic for which it stands, one Nation under God, indivisible, with liberty and justice for all. Thank you, your Honor. And, thank you ladies and gentlemen of this fine jury."

Chandler bowed low as if it was the final act of a Broadway stage production then walked confidently back to his table and took his place.

"Thank you, Mr. Chandler," said Judge Lawson through his moustache.

Jack thought he looked a bit like a walrus.

"Mr. Bannister, you may proceed when you are ready."

6

Sam puttered about the kitchen making peppermint tea for Sandra. She sat in the large brown rocker next to the window overlooking the Minneapolis skyline. She liked to look at the steeples up and over the other constructs, which spoke of the spiritual heritage of the city, something that seemed to be lacking in recent times.

"I'm quite capable of making my own tea, you know," Sandra quipped. "Plus, the doctor said I need to get back to my normal routines as quickly as possible."

"Sure," said Sam. "You want some toast with your tea?"

"No, Sam. You need to get going."

"Cap'n Conner is totally fine with me not coming in this week at all, but you're right, I probably should. We have a lot going on, and now I want to see those jerks get busted that did this to you."

"Oh, Sam, would you check in on Maria and the kids? Zach is still in recovery mode. See if they need anything or if there's something we can do for them."

"Sure thing."

Sam brought over the tea and kissed Sandra on the forehead. "You just get better, ya?"

"I am and I will. I'm fine. Get your butt outta here!"

"Ok, ok, I'll head into the office and stop by the Davidson's on my way home."

"Be careful out there, Sam. It's a weird time."

"You got that right, honey," Sam replied. "I will." And then added, "You know me" to which Sandra replied, "That's what I'm worried about!"

Sam donned his coat and little flat cap, a soft tweed topper with a small front bill, and headed out into the brisk wind of November 17th.

As he got into his car, he thought he noticed Asaph, Zach's son at the end of the block with some other guys. *Maybe his team.* He watched for a moment and didn't like the 'feel' he got from the cohort. He made a note to himself to talk to Ace the next time he saw him.

Franklin Hanover and A.J. Davis boarded the King Air 200 twin-engine aircraft and found their seats accordingly. It was a short flight to Quito.

Davis had some trouble working his seatbelt while the flight attendant went through the mandatory instructions in Spanish. Every once in a while, Davis would look up and nod. Then the seatbelt clicked into place and he settled.

"Hey boss, do you mind running over the game plan again?"

Hanover stretched his neck to look around. He felt safe enough to talk in a low whisper.

"Cain is a player. He loves his wealth, his history, and his art - and that's his weakness. We know his organization and his side-hustles all have an antisemitic underbelly and we have reason to believe he was the moneybags behind the Yetterman murder as well as a few others. He may even had something to do with the assassination attempt on President Walters but we don't know that for sure. What we have in our hands in that little briefcase of ours is a near-perfect reproduction of one of the Jewish masterpieces stolen by the Nazis in the Holocaust of WWII plus some sketches by Hitler's favourite artist. When he sees them, he will want them. That's for sure. We should be able to bait him into further conversations and if we're lucky, get him to admit some of his involvement. That's what we have so far."

"A lot of variables in there," Davis noted.

"Always is. A little bit of skill, a little bit of luck and we get our man," said Hanover.

The two of them pressed back into their seats and waited for the pretzels and complimentary coffee.

Davis looked around him and had to stop himself from profiling passengers.

Might as well just enjoy this.

Hanover leaned over and said to his partner, "You know, Davis, Adolf Hitler, among other things, was a criminal genius, an art thief and an incredible motivational speaker - but it was all for evil purposes."

Davis nodded his agreement.

"Wasn't he an artist himself?" Davis asked.

"A legend in his own mind, but he was denied admission to the Vienna Academy of Fine Arts - and therein lies one of the wounds that drove him.

"He thought of himself as an art connoisseur of sorts, and in his Mein Kampf manifesto, he attacked modern art as degenerate."

"He was the degenerate, said Davis. I don't even understand how the guy made it into government."

"He gave the people what they wanted - success. They wanted to be the most influential and aristocratic people on the planet, and he sold them a bill of goods saying they were better than everybody else. Once he became Chancellor in '33, he simply enforced his own views and there was nothing anyone could do about it. Quite horrific."

"Quite horrific that people are doing the same things today," said Davis.

"Nothing new under the sun, Agent Davis, nothing new."

Frank turned to look out the window as the King Air 200 began to taxi to its take-off.

He breathed deeply. *It's gonna be a good day.*

Sam arrived at the precinct and offered pleasantries to several of the members as he headed to his third-floor office. He caught one of the officers propping up a miniature Palestinian green and white flag on the corner of his desk as he walked by. Sam stopped.

He looked at the flag and at the officer, who was older than Sam but had less time on the force.

"Anything you want to say to me," Sam asked.

"No. Not a thing," Devon Fletcher retorted but he spun the little flag pole between his fingers, causing the flag to spin round and round. "Not right now, anyway."

Sam shook his head and muttered, "Anytime" but stepped away and continued toward the stairway in the corner of the room.

"Palestinian flag colours match the Horses of the Apocalypse, did you know that?" Fletcher called out after him.

Sam ignored him and bounded up the stairs.

Getting to his office felt like a bit of a refuge. He sat in his oversized leather chair and spun it toward the view of the city. Leaning back he remembered Braxton's letter, still folded in his inside suit jacket pocket.

"... I didn't know how empty I was inside until I listened to the preacher that day. Then I couldn't get it outta my head. Maybe you understand some of this because you taught me some things from the Good Book as well - about that guy named Haman in the Book of Esther.

That was the ironic thing that happened that day. You'd never guess what the preacher was talking about... yep, Haman but he used it as a template for not only what is happening in our world today with this growing antisemitism, but also as a way of explaining the bigger picture - that the spirit of Haman, as he called it, is still alive and well, but bigger than we think - that it wants to destroy the seed of God, which in the end boils down to you know, Jesus Christ.

Sorry, man, I'm rambling. Or maybe I'm preaching! Wow! Sorry. I'm still trying to process all of this. Hope you don't mind. You're kind of the only one I know I can talk to about stuff like this.

Oh, and I get that you are Jewish and probably not that familiar with this Jesus cat, though he was Jewish too. Lol.

Sam looked at the files in front of him.

He's reaching out. I need to email him this afternoon.

And one file was beckoning him from down under.

7

David C. Cain boarded his chartered flight from Quito to San Antonio, Texas with only a carry-on. In his mind, he was already planning his next escape to another paradise, probably Barbados but he was due back in New York for some meetings. He considered board meetings to be a necessary evil, rubber stamping his every desire, as his board members were paid a great deal of money under the table to be his yes-men. But there was one gala event he was looking forward to - an art auction fundraiser for his charity.

His organization, the People for Victims of Injustice (PVI) a non-governmental organization (NGO), often working closely with the United Nations, had been a front for antisemitism and anti-Zionist efforts for years, all under the guise of goodwill and the cause of human rights. Cain was good at what he was - a pretender and chameleon. He knew it and liked what he was getting away with.

He could hobnob with the best that society had to offer, donning black tux and tails and solving world problems over champagne with the rich and famous and it never occurred to him that there was something wrong with that picture in and of itself. It never occurred to any of them. But the discussions often focused on poorer countries needing food and fresh water, and there were numerous projects that the PVI were directing and directly responsible for, good works for fellow human beings, he would say. And the people lapped it up.

He had no problem twisting and manipulating some of those leaders of poorer countries, those who were desperate enough to bow to outside pressure from such groups, governmental, and non-governmental organizations (NGOs) alike such as the PVI. Exhaustion often led to desperation and desperation led to deception. Bowing at times meant actions like curtailing births in exchange for financial assistance, or receiving humanitarian aid if, and only if, they enforced certain governmental resolutions, or even going so far as to ensure specific people groups were flushed out of their country in exchange for a supply of food and fresh water with help, of course, from the PVI.

Cain had worked hard to obtain what he enjoyed. He attained his position of president of the PVI easily enough, developing the NGO himself with the help of his small board of directors, which only met a couple of times a year. But moving his way in and out of the offices and homes of the most influential and wealthy people on the planet came with some sacrifices too, though in his mind, it wasn't sacrificial at all.

He no longer had much connection with his blood family, most of whom lived in Amarillo, Texas. He was not married since that kind of commitment simply went against his better judgment. He loved and used women all the time, but didn't want to commit to any of them.

His mother and father, Peter and Amanda Cain, and his three siblings, Peter Jr., Jonathan and Candy were distant at best. They would all call themselves evangelical Christians but had such staunch and rigid views that David couldn't hold on to them early in life. Those beliefs mostly had to do with heaven and hell, judgment and accountability, privilege and poverty etc., and so he separated himself from them as soon as he could after high school, fleeing north to Colorado, and then to New York to carve out his own trail, which he did. His parents eventually liked what he seemed to be accomplishing but they didn't like his lack of faith.

He started with nothing, but now lived high on the hog, as they say, as well off as anyone. He was seen as a philanthropist and helper of humanity; he was fit, hardly drank at all except when he needed to blend in at gatherings. And, he was good at what he did. Why shouldn't he be pleased? Yet despite taking pride in his good deeds for all of humanity, he still couldn't shake his deep inner hatred for Jewish people in particular. Even he didn't know exactly why he retained his bitterness.

He used to blame the Jews for killing Christ, just like his parents and their brand of Christianity had taught him, but in his mind, *everybody killed Christ.*

And so, he gave up the Christ-killers theory years ago yet still held on to the hatred, which grew and intensified from there. There were times when the hate overwhelmed him as if some outside force was pressing in on him to take certain actions, sometimes good actions resulting in more favour with the higher-ups. He even felt 'inspired' at times by his pro-humanity ideas that were ultimately aimed against the humanity of Israel. He had worked hard on as many human rights committees as he could get on, especially ones governed by the UN, and he had a passion for the Palestinian people, convinced that they were always on the evil end of a nasty big stick in the strong right arm of Israel.

As the PVI organization got off its feet, he found many people had the same drive and the same 'inspiration' as he had, and those people often came with big dollars. The money started rolling in. It wasn't long before David C. Cain justified his lifestyle for all his good deeds.

He never wanted to see his family again. He felt he was better off without their influence. He just lived for himself day by day. He glanced out the window at the tropical landscape of Quito, Ecuador.

Yet here I am… off to Texas, the Lone Star State and home of the truly brave and truly free.

He breathed deeply and let out a long sigh as his charter taxied down one runway at Mariscal International, while a King Air 200 twin prop airbus touched down on another, and FBI Agents Hanover and Davis prepared to deboard.

Jack Bannister rose.

"Thank you, Your Honour."

He stepped out from behind the Defence table, with David Rabinowitz watching his every move, as was the jury.

He managed four steps toward center stage in front of the Bench before stopping as if deep in thought.

"Members of the Jury, you have heard testimony from the defendant Mr. Rabinowitz of his whereabouts that fateful day back in April. You've heard the damning expert witnesses of the prosecution say the fingerprints on the rifle that was conveniently found in a nearby parking lot, were, in fact, his, no question. We're not arguing against that - the weapon was indeed found near the shooter's perch, and it did have his fingerprints on it. But the question is: how did his fingerprints get on that rifle? If David, I mean, Mr. Rabinowitz, was such an expert marksman, an assassin as it were - and whoever shot that gun was an expert, perhaps even missing his - or her - target on purpose - just my opinion - would he or she then be so sloppy as to dump the murder weapon in a nearby underground parking lot garbage bin not 500 yards away? C'mon. That argument was all a little too easy, a little too convenient if you will. David has been an activist for Israel, yes, and has a few misdemeanours under his belt but has never been arrested for any violent act, ever. How does one go from walking in a few peaceful marches to taking a long-distance shot at the president of the United States? Is that even a concept based on reality? I don't think so, but of course, you're the ones who have to decide David's fate here, aren't you?"

Jack walked over to the Jury's box and leaned on the oak railing separating them from everyone else in the courtroom. He looked up and down the two rows, meeting the eyes of each juror. He even cast his glance at the alternate jurors, though they likely wouldn't play a part.

"Ladies and gentlemen, in this country, we still believe in the innocence of people until they are proven guilty - without a shadow of doubt. And believe me, there are many shadows here. We know that David spent a bit of time in the U.S. Army Reserves and was indeed trained by the U.S. Military in firearms, even had some limited marksmanship success in his service, but that was many years ago and to execute a shot like that - even hitting the shoulder of Madam President, amid the everyday distractions of the city of Washington D.C. through high winds atop a ten story building, through traffic and crowds, and again - to actually hit the president in the shoulder and then fire a couple of random shots up, out and away like some wild-armed pitcher on a baseball mound... well, that's a bit far fetched. There are no records of him, no evidence of him having kept up his military training, no

Saturdays or Sundays spent target practicing at the gun range, no stints down to the local sportsman's shop to see what's new in firearms. He had no weapons of any kind in his apartment, and no evidence of gunpowder residue on his fingers. Further, the shooter had to be right-handed from where he or she had been positioned by the air conditioning unit because it would be virtually impossible for him to bend his left elbow at 90 degrees to even pull the trigger properly according to where the shells fell and the footprints pressed in on the pea gravel on the roof. And oh, did I mention this? Poor ol' David over there on the defendant's chair - he's left-handed through and through. All through grade school, and middle school, as a freshman and in senior high, he threw a baseball, wrote, and blew kisses with his left hand. We have submitted photos of all that as you know.

"Additionally, his military records show that as a marksman, David Rabinowitz pulled every trigger he ever pulled with his left index finger, on his left hand, to be clear, and entered competitions as a left-handed marksman. Do you think it's possible that in just a few short years, he could have retrained his brain and all his bodily abilities, his muscle memory, to shoot right-handed? And to pull off a shot like the one that took place back in April against our president? Shadows, ladies and gentlemen, merely shadows."

Jack walked back to the front of the bench. Every eye in the courtroom, including David's parents, Mr. & Mrs. Jonathan Rabinowitz, and even the paintings on the wall seemed fixed on him.

"I'll admit that it is possible that David Rabinowitz pulled off this incredible shooting display and it's possible that he was then as stupid as the prosecution wants us to believe to leave his fingerprints and even the weapon as it was found… it's possible but not probable. And wise men and wise women base their lives on probabilities, my friends, probabilities not possibilities. Probabilities."

Jack took a deep breath, put his hands behind his back and stretched.

"Ladies and gentlemen, I ask you, are you wise people?"

He turned to look at David.

"And, if you recall, the so-called 'eye witness' accounts of seeing David down there in the vicinity of the shooting that day, have remarkably disappeared, perhaps paid off or maybe done away with, we don't know, and may never know, but they were recorded on paper by investigators, and all over the media, just never seemed to live to show up in this courtroom, did they? Shadows. The fact that this entire country has suffered an incredible inflammation of anti-Israeli sentiment and violence against Jewish people like never before, right after David was arrested may point to a bigger picture going on here, a bigger story going on here that says something else. But, that's not why we're here, are we? We don't have to explain all that or talk about the ripple effect of the Gaza war. We're here to deal with Mr. David Rabinowitz, who was arrested at his apartment the same day of the shooting, where he had spent his entire day working on his computer, and was totally shocked when the Brute Squad came crashing through his door. More shadows, my friends. Let's base our lives on reality, folks, not shadows. I thank you for your time and know that you are wise people and you will make the right decision here today, for all those concerned."

Judge Lawson let Jack get back to his place with his client before proceeding.

"Thank you, Mr. Bannister and thank you, Mr. Chandler for your summations. That concludes the submissions to this court."

He directed his attention to the jurors.

"It is now over to you, members of the jury, to do your utmost, your level best to impart true justice in the matter of the State versus David Rabinowitz. You are hereby sequestered until you arrive at a unanimous decision, guilty or not guilty. May justice prevail. Thank you."

He banged his gavel hard on the great oak bench.

"All rise!" the bailiff barked.The sound of wooden chairs on wooden floors resounded like the sound of an angry elephant as everyone stood and the Judge exited out toward his chambers. Then it was mayhem as reporters rushed to give their updates, and those in the gallery began to exit.

Kyle Owen walked over to Rabinowitz, who held out his wrists in submission. Kyle did his duty with a bit of a bored look on his face and led him back to his cell.

Jack looked over to the prosecution side of the room. Brandon Chandler appeared pensive as he took a sip of water and put his belongings back in the briefcase. He glanced at Jack, who nodded & smiled.

Chandler quickly looked away but Jack thought he perceived a slight, albeit very slight nod, even as he turned away.

8

Sam's eye caught the sticker tab of the file marked G. W. Tennyson. He pulled it to his lap, flipped it open and perused the notes.

Geoffrey Wittman Tennyson, 38, Australian-born, murdered in his apartment at 226 Albertson Way on November 26, 2024.

Time: Approximately 10 p.m.

Cause of death: Stabbed 12 times.

Motive: Robbery. Empty wallet by the body. Alcohol spilled on the rug. Open and shut.

The statement was signed by investigating officer Devon Fletcher.

Sam sighed.

Do I want to take this on? He took a sip of his coffee and closed his eyes. He knew that to go against Fletcher's findings would cause fireworks in some way, but part of him was in the mood for a fight if a fight was warranted. He thought he would take a closer look at the case. The file had some further documents and photos that Sam looked at. He scratched his nose and bit his bottom lip as he pondered the spilled alcoholic beverage beside Tennyson's body. Something wasn't clicking for him but he couldn't put his finger on it.

He got up from his chair, pulled the file together, took another sip of his coffee and grabbed his coat.

Shelly Davidson strolled along the sidewalk toward her father's store, which was still closed while he recovered.

A white van with darkened windows drove up beside her and ambled along at her pace. The window went down electronically and a bearded man leaned out.

"Hey kid, do you know where Davidson's store is?"

Shelly stopped. The van stopped.

"Yes. It's about a block further. It's my dad's store. But it's not open."

"Oh, we're not looking to buy anything." The man turned and looked at the driver and both laughed out loud. "You say it's your dad's store, eh?"

Shelly now alerted, didn't answer but started walking again but faster. The van sped up and the man got out almost upon her.

She screamed and ran and tucked into a kid-sized space between two fences that she and her friends used as a shortcut to the alley back of the store

"C'mon kid, we just want to talk!"

Shelly kept running without looking back.

The man jumped back into the van which sped up the street then turned in at the alley to the right of the store and parked about 30 metres down. They were not focused on little girls anymore, though Shelly saw them as she scuttled across the alley toward the back door of their house.

The two men sashayed like peacocks toward the main street and brazenly stood in front of the store, each with a Molotov cocktail in hand. They lit them.

One threw the flammable explosive right through the plate glass window, dropping shards of glass to the street and immediately causing an alarm to sound. It was 3:35 p.m. but no one seemed to be bothered.

The other man, dressed in a long overcoat, threw the his cocktail through the empty space further and deeper into the store.

And with that, Zach's store soon became inflamed.

Shelly burst through the back screen door of the residence yelling, "Mommy, Mommy!"

Maria rushed into the kitchen area from the living room and said, "What is it, child?"

"I was chased by some men. Scary men! And I think they are at the store right now!"

"Ok, ok. Calm down now. You're ok. What do you mean they're at the store?"

That was right when the alarm went off and Maria screamed. She rushed back to the living room where Zach was on the couch, doing ok, but still in recovery mode, as every movement of his body seemed to cause pain somewhere.

"What is it?" Zach squeaked out. "What's going on? Is that the store alarm?"

"Yes, some guys may be breaking in or something."

Zach instinctively swung his legs off the couch and sat upright and then paused and winced as the pain shot through his upper body. He groaned.

He stood up and and slipped on some loafers. He was in sweatpants and a T-shirt.

"What are you doing?" Maria demanded. "You're not going anywhere."

Just then, the white van sped by the side window going way too fast for a back alley.

"This is going bad fast. Call the cops," Zach said as he moved past Maria and went out the back door. He heard the alarm and saw smoke billowing out front.

"Call the fire department first. Or just call 911. We've got a fire!"

The fire department wasn't too long in arriving but they could not save the store. They did, however, save the residential area in the back as well as the surrounding buildings.

Ace came home from basketball practice to find the store gutted and smouldering and his family sitting on lawn chairs across the street watching its demise. He raced across the road.

"What the heck?" Ace said, hands out. "What happened?"

"It was targeted. Shelly was almost abducted," said Maria.

"What?!" The anger and thirst for revenge bubbled up inside Ace more than ever and he couldn't control himself.

He let out a guttural scream.

"I'm going to kill somebody! If I find out who did this, they're dead!"

Zach and Maria hugged their boy and let him vent for a bit.

"That's only going to get you killed, Ace. But I understand your anger. This has gone way too far," said Zach.

"It's everywhere I turn, Dad. I mean, if I wasn't good at basketball, I'd probably be fighting off idiots all the time. Everyone seems to hate us. What have we done?"

"I know, son, it's a fearful thing to wear a kippah anywhere in the world these days."

"What are we supposed to do now? The store's gone. Our heritage is gone…our income is gone!"

"Our heritage is not gone Ace; our heritage, our way is to fight and survive through adversity. My father and his father before him struggled every day to carve out a life for us. My grandfather was murdered in Auschwitz and my mother and my father were survivors though they didn't know each other then. They survived. They lived. That is what we do."

Zach smiled at his boy and added, "Like the old saying goes, Ace, 'they tried to kill us; we survived. Let's eat.' C'mon, let's go back to the house with your mother and sister."

The small family walked back arm in arm amidst the lines of hoses and neighbourhood gawkers, down the side alley and in through the back screen door. The smell of smoke and plastics filled the air.

Zach put his arm around his wife.

"We're okay. That's all that matters."

9

Jack Bannister felt the proceedings went as he had hoped and anticipated. Loose ends around the expertise of the shooter, and any motive that his client might have to take out the president seemed dubious at best.

It was 6 p.m. He didn't think the jury would be done deliberating until late night or early morning. He was deciding on whether to go back to his hotel and rest a bit before a late dinner or just find a nice restaurant to settle into when his phone buzzed.

"Jack here," he said.

"Hey, Jack, it's Tony."

Tony Gaffey was the court clerk, whom Jack considered a 'good man' as he often told his colleagues when they needed some inside information or help.

"The jury is done, man! It's over! The Judge is looking to come back in at 8 p.m. I was not expecting that!"

"Nor was I my friend, thanks for letting me know."

"Hey, well that's my job to let you lawyers know, but I also wanted to let you know first. I think it may be a good omen for you," Tony said. "Gotta make some more calls. See ya!"

The phone went dead and Jack stuck it back into his pocket, looked at his watch and thought *time for a quick bite.*

He stopped in at The Runway, a small trendy bistro that was easily accessible when coming out of Reagan National, the closest airport to downtown D.C.

It was a typical long-countered bistro designed with a 60's theme but served more than just hot drinks and snacks. It also had a variety of sandwiches off the grill and hearty soups. Jack ordered a decaf Americano, beef barley soup and a bun.

He was back at the courthouse within an hour.

The media mobs gathered around the hallways like scavenger birds on a carcass. Jack sat on a bench outside the courtroom door and waited, eyeing the various media personalities, some famous and some wanting to be famous, making their mark in the dog-eat-dog world of cutthroat journalism.

Mr. & Mrs. Rabinowitz walked in and Jack rose to meet them.

He heard the click of the lock in the door at 7:35 p.m. and Tony Gaffey swung the door open with a nod and half-smile to Jack, who returned the gesture.

The mob rushed in to find their seats and the Rabinowitzs moved quickly as well but Jack waited, knowing his seat was secure. He breathed deeply and walked through the doors.

~

"All rise."

Kyle Owen stood at his post by the big door, hand on his sidearm as Judge Bryce Lawson entered the room.

"You may be seated," said the Colonel Custer look-alike. "This court is back in session." He banged his gavel like he meant it.

"The defendant will please rise. Has the jury reached a verdict?" Lawson asked the foreperson of the 12.

Susan Hawthorne, a high school science teacher, rose to meet the judge's request and cleared her throat.

"We have, Your Honor," she said. "On the charge of Attempted Murder, the jury finds the defendant… not guilty."

A cacophony went up from the gallery, everything from gasps to claps, to boos and cheers. The gavel came down hard again, as Judge Bryce Lawson spoke over the noise, "Order! Order in this courtroom!" The crowd noise dimmed a bit and a few media reps slipped out with a bow and their back to the door. Rabinowitz shook Jack's hand and pulled him in for a broad embrace.

"You may continue, Ms. Hawthorne."

"On the charge of Conspiracy to Commit Murder, the jury finds the defendant... not guilty."

Rabinowitz looked up and breathed a "thank God" and the crowd noise rose again above it all and the gavel came down hard again.

Mrs. Rabinowitz pretty much fainted into her husband's arms and they both sat down with tears in their eyes.

"Thank you ladies and gentlemen of the jury! You are officially dismissed at this point. Mr. Rabinowitz, there will be some paperwork to complete but for all intents and purposes, you are a free man!"

The gavel came down two more times.

"This court stands adjourned!"

Mayhem broke out as the rest of the reporters shot out of the room. David Rabinowitz looked at Jack and held out both hands in a gesture of a shrug as if to say, "What now?"

"Your friend, Kyle, there, will take you back to your cell for the night, but you'll be out of here by noon tomorrow. Congratulations, David."

"I don't know how to thank you, Jack. You're an amazing lawyer."

"Keep your nose clean," said Jack, and reached out his hand again and shook the young man's hand. Kyle came over and skipped the handcuffs but led David out the side door. Jonathan Rabinowitz came over to thank Jack and shake his hand.

"Thank you, Jack. You're the best," Rabinowitz said.

"Glad to be able to help," said Jack.

The Rabinowitzs were the last to leave before Jack.

He paused and sat down again for a moment in the quiet courtroom. The prosecution had already left the area.

He looked at the paintings around the room and almost felt a nod of approval from the old guard.

The wheels of David Cain's charter screeched twice as they hit the tarmac of San Antonio Airport, about 30 minutes outside the city. From there it was less than an hour's flight to Rick Husband International Airport in Amarillo, Texas. Cain stayed on board while the jet was refuelled and various maintenance tasks were completed and entered into the log.

He began to think about his parents, at first with disdain, then anger, then pity started to rise inside him. He even caught himself thinking about how he had hurt them over the years. He shook himself out of that process and got the steward to bring him a bit of seasonal fruit to eat and a diet drink. He needed to stay alert, be focused and on his A-game if he was to engage in familial conversation.

Special Agents Hanover and Davis could not believe their ears.

Juan Juarez, the 23-year-old managerial apprentice at the Grand Talisman Hotel & Suites was adamant.

"He is gone, señor. He is like Elvis. He has left the building." He smiled at his little joke.

Frank didn't bother pulling out his badge. They had come in with the story that they were old friends and were trying to track down Cain, had a gift for him.

Juarez shrugged and smiled and did his best to look as innocent as possible, adding, "I can take the gift and hold it for him."

Frank tapped his right-hand fingers on the front desk.

"Ok. I'm going to jot a little message for him here on this paper. Will you make sure it gets to him when he comes back?"

"Si, si señor no problemo. If he comes back. He just shows up from time to time and we have a suite in reserve for him. He is a very good guest."

AJ chimed in: "that's a little unusual isn't it?" Frank nudged him with his elbow as if to say, *"Too investigator-like."*

But Juarez just smiled and rubbed his thumb and forefinger together.

They knew what he was saying.

Frank finished writing his note and hoped that Cain would get it, maybe taking the bait about what the briefcase held in store for him if he was interested. But both agents knew he was long gone and they didn't have a clue as to where.

10

Detective Sam Silverman walked up to the door of Geoffrey Tennyson's apartment. It still had police tape across the door, which he ducked under after using the keys in the case file to enter.

He closed the door behind him, put little cloth slippers over his feet and donned tight blue synthetic gloves. He would walk the grid as he had learned from Braxton, taking each step very slowly and carefully, "old school" as some would say, looking up and down, side to side, wall to wall, and ceiling to floor.

The outline of the body was still on the carpeted floor as well as the stain of alcohol.

"Who were you, Geoffrey Wittman Tennyson?" Sam started processing out loud.

He studied the decor. It was simple but clean. He noticed books on the living room shelves, The Fall of Rome, Hitler's Mein Kampf, Pagan Christianity, George Orwell's 1984, The Holy Bible, and The Collected Works of Edgar Allen Poe.

"An intelligent dude, that's for sure."

He made his way into the first of two bedrooms. The first was a guest room, nicely decorated with a queen bed on one side and a large wooden wardrobe on the other. He opened the wardrobe.

"No Narnia," he said out loud with a smile. *Nothing else either.*

He looked up and down the walls and in the drawers under the bed. *Nothing.* He moved to the kitchen, which was separated from the living room by a large butcher block island. The living room was where the body was found. His phone buzzed.

"Hey babe!"

"Hi, Sam."

"Everything okay? Are you alright?"

"Yes, absolutely. I just wanted you to pick up a few things at the market before you come home. Where are you?"

"Oh," said Sam. "I'm just taking a little look at a new case, supposedly open and shut, but something's bugging me."

"There's always something bugging you," Sandra laughed, proud of her policeman husband.

"What do you need? I'll come home after this."

As Sam took down Sandra's list of items, he thought about Zach and his family, having learned of the fire. He shook his head at the trauma that they have had to endure lately. *Need to stop by and see them soon, too.*

He finished his conversation with Sandra with a "love you," and put the phone back on his belt.

As he stepped out of the one bedroom and looked at the kitchen, he fixated on the island. The island seemed a little overbearing to him, and he noted that the countertop was fake butcher block wood as it was peeling away on one corner.

He slowly walked down the side of the island, running one finger along the edge, moved toward the fridge, and opened it. *Still full of normalcy.* He reached for one cupboard, then the next, and the next. Then he pulled the drawers and opened the cupboards under the island.

That's when it hit him.

There was not a single bottle of hard alcohol or beer in the entire apartment.

It was a brisk but bright November morning.

"Congratulations, David, you are a free man."

Jennifer Dawson, the 34-year-old Washington D.C. Courthouse receptionist looked kindly up from the front desk of the Courthouse with Kyle Owen standing casually nearby.

David Rabinowitz looked back at Kyle and nodded with a slight smile and gave a salute to the officer.

Kyle smiled and saluted back. "Good luck, David. Congratulations, man."

Jack Bannister placed the final signature on the paperwork in front of them and made a humorous comment to Ms. Dawson. He and David then moved toward the brightness of the awaiting day.

Jack held the door open for David, almost like in a grand ceremony, and David smiled as he walked through.

"Freedom!" He fake-yelled as if he was William Wallace on the fields of Bannockburn in Scotland ready to face the English. The two of them laughed as they moved toward the top of the stairs.

"All you need is a little blue face paint," Jack quipped.

A couple of reporters with cameras took some candid shots and one asked the proverbial, "How do you feel, David?" But the larger mob of media were long gone.

He paused and responded with a wide-grinned "Feel? I feel awesome!"

Mr. and Mrs. Rabinowitz stood back and let David enjoy the moment. They smiled and clapped and watched with joy. The lightness of the moment was shattered though, by a crowd with green and white protest signs coming loudly from across the courtyard. The signs were about Palestinian freedom and gassing the Jews. David wrinkled up his mouth into a sneer and looked at Jack, who was steely-eyed and squinting.

David winced with indigestion of his morning breakfast but realized it wasn't indigestion when he saw the spreading red bloodspot on his pale blue shirt. He grabbed his gut with a whispered grunt like he was lifting something heavy.

Another bullet hit him in the middle of his chest and he fell backwards on the steps. Mrs. Rabinowitz screamed and ran toward her son with her husband right behind.

Jack heard no shots and wondered what had happened. The reporters gasped and swung their cameras toward the crowd, looking for a shooter. Seeing none, they tracked back to David Rabinowitz bleeding on the cement stairs. Jack knelt beside David and watched the bloodspots increasing on his torso as he held his head in his hands.

"Aw David," said Jack. "I'm sorry, man, so sorry. Hang in there. We're calling 911 right now. Ambulance will be here in a second."

The Rabinowitzs could not believe what was happening and Mrs. Rabinowitz wailed loudly in protest.

David breathed deeply, smiled a little smile, and spurted blood from his mouth. He said something unintelligible to Jack, and then he was gone.

Later that evening in Minneapolis, Sandra had retired early for the night and was resting easy. Sam sat in his recliner and thought about Geoffrey Tennyson.

What were you up to, Mr. Tennyson? Who would want to kill you if.. if robbery wasn't the motive? And if robbery is not the motive, what was the motive? You were not a drinker, were you? There are no receipts in your home for any alcohol whatsoever. There are no reports of you down at the corner pub, making a fool of yourself, nor were you known at the liquor store. No other bottles in your cupboards, yet there was half a bottle of Jameson's Irish Whiskey spilled all over your carpet and the other half was in your bloodstream. What is going on? What happened that night?

The vibrating buzz of his phone made him jump. He rolled his eyes and looked at his screen.

Oliver Braxton.

Well, I'll be!

He hit the green button and whispered with quiet excitement, "Oliver! Wow, good to hear from you. Sandra's sleeping so I can't talk too loud. Let me just move into another room."

"That's cool, bro," said Oliver. "I'm just checking in to see how she's doing, and how you're doing too. Got any big cases going on?"

"Just a sec."

Sam tiptoed past the bedroom door and down the hall to a little den of sorts. He went in and shut the door.

"Did you get my letter?" Oliver asked.

"Yes I did, but to be honest, with the shooting, and recovery and work, I've only read half of it!"

"Ha ha, that's alright. Maybe it's one of those timing things, ya know?"

"Sure, sure, how are you doing, boss?"

"Still call me boss? I'm doing good, better than ever really," said Oliver. "I've been going to this big ol' Presbyterian Church downtown and..."

"Ya I know the one," chirped Sam.

"Ya, and well, it has been real good for me; they got this course going on dealing with the big questions of life and well, I've got a few of them, you know? But it's been good."

"Wow. I'm happy for you, Brax. I really am. Sandra's doing well, just tired as her body's recovering. It doesn't like getting shot, eh?"

They both laughed at that comment. Braxton recalled taking a slug to his upper thigh one time that took him out for almost five months of his policing career.

"I'm glad to hear she's doing good," he said. "Tell her I said hi, and give her a hug for me."

"Absolutely. So, you asked about cases."

"Ya ya, my life's pretty quiet now as I move toward retirement, mostly sitting at a desk and sorting papers for the *el Capitan,* you remember Red don't you?"

"Of course, bringing back some fond memories boss," Sam chuckled.

"But ya, I'm working on this one. Maybe you have some thoughts. A man, Geoff Tennyson, well Geoffrey officially, was murdered in his home, made to look like a robbery in my opinion, but I can't find a real motive. The scene looks to be a setup - alcohol in his body and all around him, yet he wasn't known to be a drinker."

"Hmm," said Braxton closing his eyes and picturing the crime scene.

"Not a trace of any other alcoholic beverages in his house, no bottles, no receipts, no labels, no recycling - well, there was recycling but only diet pop cans and health drinks. I think there's more here than meets the eye."

Sam could hear the resistance of Oliver's chair as he leaned back on it as far as it would go.

"You're going to snap that thing, Brax!" Sam laughed.

"Ha ha, you're probably right. Hey, let me do some digging. It's all I do now anyway. What's his name again?"

"Tennyson. Geoffrey Wittman Tennyson. He was 38. Seems clean cut but maybe there's some other connection somewhere. Oh and Brax…"

"Yep, I'm listening."

"The initial investigating officer was a cop named Devon Fletcher. He's a total racist - always jabbing at me about being Jewish and freeing Palestine etc. For me to pick this up after he signed off on it… well, let's just say it's going to ruffle his feathers a bit."

"You be careful, Sam. There's so much crap hitting the fan these days that you may just get splattered if you're not smart."

"Oh, I'm careful, boss. But thanks. Hey, and thanks for the call. Great to hear your voice again."

"Haha, you bet. Oliver Braxton on the job. I'll get back to you if I find anything significant with Tennyson."

11

Sam hung up the phone and went back into the living room. He walked across the coffee-coloured carpet toward the front door where he hung his coat. Reaching into the inner pocket, he pulled out Oliver's letter that he had yet to finish and sat down in his big grey recliner, kicked the footrest out and unfolded the two-pager to where he had left off.

The big old Presbyterian Church is pretty famous, had some famous preachers. But anyway, it all seemed to be tweaked toward people like me - you know, raised in the church but then left the church, then had some crisis, then wandered back into the church. The music is contemporary and well done - you know how I enjoy classical - and they seemed to know their stuff. Some good musicians. In fact, there seemed to be an abundance of artist types in the building that morning, actors and whatnot. They had some art exhibit thing going on too.

Anyway, I wanted to tell you that my spiritual side is flickering or being awakened or something. Figured you'd understand given your heritage and attending synagogue and all. It all feels new to me, but so far, so good.

Hope you're doing well.

Keep in touch, bro

Ollie

Sam looked at the signature and realized that he'd never heard the nickname "Ollie" before. Brax had never mentioned it and he wouldn't have dared suggest it for his boss. He always called him "Boss" or "Chief" or "sir."

He folded up the letter, thinking about Braxton being called Ollie and also 'religious'. *I suppose it works.*

Sam pushed down the footrest with the weight of his feet and stood up.

Need to get to bed. Gotta get up early tomorrow.

It was a bright mid-winter's-morning when a vocal mob carrying placards and flags surrounded an elderly Jewish couple as they left the synagogue in New York City.

They walked briskly alongside the couple and shouted obscenities at them.

The woman, dressed in her Saturday best, was pressing into the arm and shoulder of her 72-year-old husband and would say back to those accosting them, "You're disgusting," and "You have no idea." The husband, wearing a Kippuh and donning a blue scarf and wool coat, had a cane in his other hand. Still, they walked as fast as they could toward the bus stop.

The crowd pushed in and didn't allow them to move forward. Cars drove by; people passed by on foot not wanting to get involved. The verbal harassment increased and a woman two-hand shoved the Jewish lady backwards.

Then, in a second, a rock came out of the air and landed squarely on the man's temple with a knocking sound that resembled a woodblock instrument used in folk music.

He went down hard on the sidewalk and his wife took a push from behind and fell on top of him. The crowd cheered but also scattered in a flash, leaving the two lying there. The man was alive but bleeding from his temple. He could hear in the distance, as if waking from a dream, "Go home Jewish dogs! We don't want you here!"

His wife was crying and holding his head in her hands as he came to and started to sit up.

The brightness of the day hurt his eyes.

❖

David C. Cain stood uncomfortably in the hallway of the BSA Hospital before opening the door to his father's room in the ICU.

He knew the history of this place, how in the early 1900s four young women from the Sisters of Charity of the Incarnate Word tried to meet the growing needs of Amarillo, but not without problems and controversy. They called their hospital St. Anthony's.

As Amarillo grew exponentially, the needs of the general public began to overwhelm St. Anthony's.

Meanwhile, their 'competitors,' the High Plains Baptist Hospital, were facing the same overwhelming odds and then in 1996 a miracle of sorts occurred when the two rivalries joined forces and became the BSA Hospital, which is now one of the largest and growing network of medical facilities, providing the best medical care while promoting Christian love, integrity and excellence.

Cain felt the encroachment of that Christian love bearing down upon him. Everywhere he looked there was a cross on a wall or a door, or plaques on the wall spouting scriptures that he once had memorized as a kid, words of Jesus of Nazareth such as, "I am the resurrection and the life, he who believes in me, though he were dead, yet shall he live." Or "I am the way, the

truth and the life, and no one comes to the
Father but by me."

Cain rolled his eyes away from that one as
he pushed open the door of Room 150 and saw
his mother's face for the first time in several
years.

"Oh David," she exclaimed. "You're here! You
came!" She immediately stood up and went to
him and embraced him in an awkward tearful
hug and he wasn't very responsive to the burst
of emotion.

"Hello... yes, yes I'm here," he said as
stoically as possible, stating the obvious. He
stepped to the left a bit and was released from
his mother's embrace.

"Your father is not doing well, David." She
began to weep and plunked down again in the
green recliner.

Cain was cringing inside from his own
emoting. He did not like to deal with his
feelings, especially when it was regarding his
parents, or his siblings. Ever since he walked
away from the Christian faith that they
represented, he has remained at a distance. He
moved to New York in a roundabout way to
escape his heritage and carve out his own trail.
He wanted nothing to do with Christian values
and he lived that out to the extreme, though at

the moment, he was feeling an obscure feeling that he knew was compassion. He didn't like it.

He looked at his father, who though asleep and unshaven looked remarkably like himself. He had never noticed that before. He blinked the thought away.

"What are the doctors saying?" He asked his mother for any more details and was glad that none of his siblings were in the room.

"Well," she said, wiping her eyes and giving her nose a little relief into a wad of tissue paper. "He's not in a coma but he's also not responsive at all, at least not very much, so he almost might as well be."

"Are they giving any sort of timeline?" David liked being blunt even though he knew it hurt his mother to talk about such things.

"Days... maybe weeks, not much more than that," she said, sitting up straight in the chair, then added with a big sigh, "David, you should talk to your siblings."

"I'd rather not. There's not really anything to talk about."

"There is planning to be done if the inevitable happens. We will need to discuss final details..."

"I don't really care what is decided. Pete and Jon and Candy can work things out. I'm not looking for anything."

"But you could be helpful."

David breathed deeply.

"Listen, I need to get back to New York... lots of things on the go... how about this: I will help in ways I can - finances and whatnot. But I don't need to see them. That just drums up emotions for everybody and none of us want to go there."

"Well, you don't know that, if you don't talk to them."

"Mom." He knew it wasn't worth the argument. She knew he wasn't going to stay. She stood up.

David tightened his lips and squared his jaw. He moved to the bed and looked closer at his dad lying there. The sound of the heart monitor grew louder.

He touched his dad's hand but pulled it away quickly.

"I've got to go. I'll be in touch."

He gave his mother a quick awkward hug and moved out of the dimly lit room and down the bright hallway toward the elevator.

He couldn't get out of there fast enough.

12

The international community was clamping down hard on Israel.

Since the Hamas War, even Canada, which was once known in Israel as 'Israel's best friend', joined a coalition of countries demanding a two-state solution to solve all of Israel's problems, though a two-state solution was no solution at all even in the minds of the enemies of Israel, let alone Israel itself. Israel had accepted and tried the two-state idea more than once before. Their enemies' solution was stated clearly in their constitutions and charters. Their solution is to wipe Israel off the map.

Special Agent Frank Hanover tried to make sense of it all as it pertained to David C. Cain. He had the file opened in front of him on the hotel desk, several photocopies and photos spread out over the entirety of the cherry-like wooden hotel table.

His eyes fixed on a two-state solution headline. He saw a problem. The Palestinian Authority (PA), which cooperated with Israel in several areas, still held to a fundamental belief that Israel should not exist. Even Egypt and Jordan, though like kindergarten classes in comparison to terrorist organizations like Hamas, still taught their children in school to hate Israel and deny Israel the right to exist. So, Israel as a whole could not and would not trust the PA despite the United States and others relying on the PA to bring peace. One report said that among Palestinians in the Middle East, the majority still felt Hamas should be the ruling power. *How could Israel trust that kind of government to be peaceful?*

Frank looked over current photos of Gaza. The area was a heap of rubble needing to be rebuilt; it resembled post-WWII Germany. However, it was that very resemblance in Frank's mind that gave some hope of a brighter future; *it can be rebuilt!* Yet no country was stepping up to provide what was needed for Gaza - no peace-keeping troops for security for citizens of Israel in the south nor even the citizens of Gaza, little finances for rebuilding roads and houses were being deployed, and food and supply trucks were still limited. Neighbouring countries were not taking refugees. What was once a beautiful strip of resorts, hotels and sandy beaches, Gaza was now a narrow band of bleakness with some 200,000 blue and white tent cities crowding the coastline, and overflowing with poverty, disease and crime. Christian and Muslim NGOs were at work in the enclave but for the most part, the world had simply turned away from the need and blamed Israel for what they called genocidal attempts, despite the very real statistics revealing an increasing population of Palestinians from the early 2000s onward. Israel was facing international isolation like never before. Across the board, from the halls of academia to the classrooms of elementary schools to the hi-tech world of science and medicine, the Jewish state has been turned into an outcast. Even the US Administration had sided with the United Nations in calling for Israel to lower their weapons against the terrorists that threatened them.

Frank pondered what he was reading and seeing. The false reports spreading like wildfire included a wide variety of topics - that Israel had attacked the Palestinians in 1948, that there were no Jewish people in the land before 1948, that Israel illegally took the land from the Arabs in 1948, and that Israel's governance of the land was a devastation to the Palestinians. *Nothing could be further from the truth.*

Frank picked up a piece of history from the table, a picture of the document signed by the United Nations when they voted in 1947 to partition the area then known as the British Mandate of Palestine into two states: one

Jewish and one Arab. The Jewish community accepted that plan and began making plans to declare statehood, but the Arab world rejected it and began preparing for war. The day after Israel declared its independence on May 14, 1948, five Arab nations gathered as one to launch a war to destroy the newborn state with the declared aim to eradicate it. Israel did not initiate the conflict but was obliged to defend itself with sticks and stones, shovels and rakes, a makeshift army, and a few planes in their airforce. Israel had no intention of destroying the Palestinian people.

As he tried to get his head around the mix of current events and history, Agent Davis walked into the room.

"Hey boss," said Davis. "Whoa, you are deep in it today!"

"You got that right, my friend. I'm trying to figure out Cain's connection to all this anti-Israel rhetoric. Why is this such a draw for him? I mean when you go through the facts, you gotta wonder what is the deal with it for most people. Israel's military responses have always been defensive against Arab aggression. Israel's military is named the Israel Defense Forces (IDF) for a reason. They're always defending themselves."

"Ya, I don't get it. But what do I know? I'm just hired from the neck down. Just tell me what to do and I do it."

Franklin looked at Davis and smiled his agreement. *That is definitely true, rookie.* Davis looked at the photos on the table.

"Whoa, that's whacked!" He said, pointing to current editorial cartoons of gross caricatures of Jewish people depicted as rats and pigs and other animals. Similar to Nazi Germany propaganda in the late 1930s and early 40s, even schools of higher education seemed bent on the destruction of Israel, using antisemitic slogans on t-shirts, posters, coffee mugs and in media. Davis seemed shocked that he was seeing the modern items of hate amongst the photos.

"The world has really turned against them," he commented.

But Frank noted there were still some standing against the hate, even at their own risk, including the country of Germany itself, which had gone above and beyond as a nation to protect and support Israel and even Jewish people abroad.

"Christians and people holding to the Christian values are holding support marches for Israel and regular rallies calling for people to "Wake Up" but what we're seeing is that society, in general, continues to footslog down a dark path of violence," Frank said. "Surprising but it's truly getting worse.

"Our job is to take out one guy who seems to be at the forefront of much of it, David C. Cain."

Sam Silverman felt the pressure.

Ever since his father died back in August, he wanted to bring his mother from Florida to live with him and Sandra. Eema Silverman wanted no part of it though, happy with her friends and the pleasant Florida weather. Sam worried that her bliss would dull her senses of any danger lurking around corners.

He also felt the atmospheric pressure of his office as sneers and jeers were a common part of his day now, even from those in the lower ranks of the police force. His brow was almost always furrowed and even his brief chats with the Captain had become less and less. He was always on his guard, and that made work exhausting - even before he began any policing.

As he worked his cases, he sensed the growing heat of the 'cauldron' as he dubbed the office, and the pressure squeezing him made his whole body *feel thin.*

His phone vibrated and he grabbed it. The display read "Ollie" ~ the name he had exchanged for 'Braxton' which he had there before.

After some pleasantries, his former partner and mentor indicated that he had picked up some interesting tidbits regarding the Tennyson case.

"It seems Mr. Tennyson there had some pro-Israel leanings and had travelled to the Holy Land in recent months on a church tour," said Brax.

"Oh? That is interesting."

"Ya, and something else. He was a cousin or second cousin or something - some kind of relative - to a man you might recall, David C. Cain. Remember him?"

"Didn't his name come up in the Yetterman file?" Sam sat up at his desk.

"Yes, it did. But that was just before we gave the file over to the FBI. We never heard nothin' after that, except the feds arresting that one guy, the racist dude…"

"Webber… Hartmann Webber."

"Ya, that guy. Cain was reportedly the bucks behind some conspiracy involving him, but the whole thing was out of our league so we just moved on," said Braxton.

"Hmm, very interesting."

"I thought you might like that."

Sam was processing out loud, "So Mr. Pro-Israel is a cousin to Mr. Anti-Israel..."

The two continued to chat about the weather in New York, the Knicks and Braxton's latest journey toward faith of some kind. Sam filled his friend in on Sandra's recovery; they spoke of the growing antisemitism and finished it off talking about Braxton's love of his old chair.

13

Cain's flight into JFK International was smooth and easy. No delays. No problems. Just the way he liked it.

He sat alone in his luxury Bentley limosine and thought about the gala fundraising event that he would host at the end of the week. It was in his mind, *epic*, a display of some of the finest and most breathtaking artistry of the modern era, including some wartime pieces known as Cubism and Dadaism, creations of a decadent 20th-century world, which he loved.

And that's what Franklin Hanover was counting on. He hoped that Cain's love for decadent art, including stolen Nazi art, would be his ultimate downfall.

Hanover looked at the briefcase beside the bed, got up from the faux leather chair and sat down on the bed, taking the briefcase in hand. He tapped the digital code to pop the two locks, which clicked up with a snap.

Opening it revealed two books and a laptop. He removed those and touched a hidden tab under the felt lining, which popped a false bottom. He lifted that and pulled out two tubes.

Popping the lid off one, he tipped out the contents and an old piece of art, about the size of a chessboard slid into his hand. He unfurled it.

"Beautiful," he said out loud though Davis wasn't there anymore. He had gone downstairs to get some ice.

Then he unfurled the rough drawings and paint markings of Adolf Ziegler's studies for his *Judgement of Paris,* a story from Greek mythology, which was one of the events that led up to the Trojan War… even the foundations of Rome. Ziegler was Adolf Hitler's favourite painter. These were hand-painted sketches and pencil drawings of the characters in the famous piece. Another tube contained more historical works.

Franklin hoped that Germanic history would draw Cain's love of art like a wiggly worm on a barbed fishing hook. When Hitler became chancellor of Germany in 1933, he enforced his particular view of fashion as well as the arts. Germany was better in so many ways, and above so much in his mind, so classical portraits and landscapes by Renaissance masters, particularly those of Germanic origin adorned the walls of every Nazi Party building. Modern artists were branded as degenerate by the Third Reich and everything they discovered in museums, estates or schools was either sold or destroyed.

The Führer's objective was to establish a European Art Museum in Linz and any money garnered from the sale of degenerate art went to that. Whenever the Nazis conquered a town or estate, all the art was confiscated and many of the SS Officers and German Commanders who took over homes grew their private collections. Frank's research revealed that Nazi theft is considered to be the largest art theft in modern history and it included paintings, furniture, sculptures, and anything in between. If it was considered to be opposing Hitler's purification of German culture, it was taken, destroyed or sold, and if it fell into Hitler's good graces, and was considered valuable, it was collected and relocated.

Not only did the Reich seize countless masterpieces from occupied territories during the war, but also put to auction a large portion of Germany's collection of great art stolen from museums and galleries. In the end, the confiscation committees removed over 15,000 works of art from German public collections.

The Reich began to collect and auction countless pieces of art— on June 30, 1939, an auction took place at the elegant Grand Hotel National in the Swiss resort town of Lucerne. All of the paintings and sculptures had been on display in museums throughout Germany. This collection offered over 100 paintings and sculptures by numerous famous artists, such as Henri Matisse, Vincent van Gogh, and Pablo Picasso, all of which were considered "degenerate" pieces by Nazi authorities and were to be banished from Germany.

All of the proceeds from the auction were deposited into "German-controlled accounts", and the museums did not receive a penny.

Frank, who needed to have an excellent working knowledge of the art and history, including the forgery he now held in his hand, was confident the ongoing resurfacing of missing or stolen art even today, along with the fight for rightful ownership, would draw Cain's attention.

His phone buzzed. It was Homeland Security.

"Hanover here."

"Sir, we have traced Cain's charter jet to JFK. Landed about an hour ago."

"Thank you."

"Sir."

Franklin ended the call and called out to his partner.

"Hey bud, we're headed to New York!"

❖

It was Friday Shabbat, a time when observing Jews quieted themselves, cooked dinner with their families, spoke gratitude and blessings over each one and invited the light of God to come and cover their weekend. Candles were lit, music was quietly serenading the two, and Sam was about to take his second bite of the supper he and Sandra had made together when the door was thumped heavily.

Sandra startled but Sam dabbed the corners of his mouth and pushed back from the table. He looked through the peephole in the door. He saw no one.

He undid the chain bolt, turned the deadlock and cracked the door. A package was on the carpeted floor in front of it. He bent down and picked it up.

Hmm. Nothing special. Brown paper, brown string. Sam shut the door and walked back to the table undoing the string as he walked.

It was Sandra who jarred him back into reality.

"What are you doing?! Don't open that. A brown paper-wrapped package? That could be a bomb!"

Sam stopped suddenly and looked at her. She was right. *What was I thinking?*

"I'm sorry," he said. "I wasn't thinking." Suddenly, he wanted the package to be anywhere but in his hands, in his home. "I'll get rid of it."

"Well, you can't just get rid of it! It could blow up in someone else's face," Sandra said. "Call somebody. Aren't there people who deal with this sort of thing?"

Sam felt ashamed and stupid that he had blanked so badly as to what to do.

"Wow. I guess I was just so into our dinner I stopped thinking like a cop," he said and apologized again. He put the package in the bathroom, shut the door and called the explosives team. They were on their way in moments.

Sam looked at his now cold dinner. *This has got to stop.*

They left and went for dinner as the team did their thing. As it turned out, a phone call two hours later informed them that it indeed had been a bomb.

"But it was a poorly made dud," the expert on the other end quickly explained. "It would have never gone off."

All the same, Sam and Sandra were both shaking as they crawled silently into bed that night.

Sandra was the first to air her feelings.

"Sam, I think it's time to consider some things."

"What things?"

"Like our lives for instance... there's so much swirling crap going on. I was almost killed while shopping. You're harassed at work by your colleagues..."

"Well, they're not really colleagues, but..."

"You know what I mean, Sam. You're focusing on my words, not my heart. I think we need... I think we need to get out."

"Get out?"

"Yes! Get out. Move. Leave. Something! We need a change. This is getting ridiculous. I cannot even walk next door without always looking over my shoulder in fear. I think of you gone all day and I'm afraid of every phone call. Sam, I want to raise a family, but not here. I do not feel safe at all here anymore, nor do many of the people we know."

She waited for Sam to process what she was saying. He was quiet and scratched his nose as he thought. He gave a big sigh. He knew she was right.

"You're probably right, well, not probably, you are right. I've been preoccupied with the case and everything, and it's getting worse every day, all around us. But I mean, the question is, where would we go?"

"You have relatives up in Canada, don't you? Or maybe we could go closer to your mom."

Both of Sandra's parents were long gone, having died in a motor vehicle accident outside of Memphis in 2013.

"I'll call my cousin tomorrow and see what's shaking up there." Sam grabbed Sandra's hand beside him and she tucked in closer to him, nuzzling into his shoulder.

"I'm sorry, Sam. But I really am scared."

"It will be ok," he said, hoping to God that he was right.

14

Ace pulled the hood up over his head as he made his way down Stafford Avenue. He was nervous but he was also intent and very focused.

Just coming off his basketball practice, he was dressed in his sweats and had kept his court shoes on. He felt strong and ready for anything. His athletic reflexes were taut; he knew he was out of his element.

Stafford was known as a high-crime area. Muggings, rapes and even murders occurred in this neighbourhood regularly. It was the 'Compton" of Minneapolis.

Dozens of people lined the sidewalks, some doing drugs, some experiencing the ups and downsides of substance abuse, some soliciting other things, and all calling out to him.

"Hey bro, why don't you come in here for a moment?"

"My man, No. 23 - are you the white Mike? Hey, nice shoes."

Two hooded teenagers stepped in pace behind Ace and were calling for his shoes.

"I likes your hoodie too bruh… you wanna sell it to me? How 'bout you just give it to me, huh?"

Ace kept his stride and though he was alert, he pretended to pay no attention to these guys. If they wanted a fight, he would fight. He fingered the flip-out box cutter knife in his hoodie pocket and pushed the unlock button. He felt the spring kick the blade out, though his stomach kept it from opening up all the way.

He saw what he was looking for: Apartment Block 420 with cement steps leading up to the main door. A group of young men and a few women sat on the stairs and held themselves as if the whole world owed them money.

He stopped in front of the gathering, wishing his sweats were not so white and purple.

The group stared at him.

They all looked rough. They all looked high, some more than others.

Ace stood strong.

"I'm looking for Jet. Anybody know Jet?"

A girl dressed in a short miniskirt and halter top, despite it being November, pulled her faux fur coat up around her shoulders.

"What you want with Jet, Mr. Athlete?"

"That's my business," said Ace. "But he told me to meet him here at 7 p.m. It's 7 p.m."

A muscled man, maybe in his early 20s, thought Ace, and decked in chains, stood up, wobbled a bit under his earlier intake of alcohol, and said, "I'm Jet. You Ace?"

"That's right. I'm Ace."

"Step into my office, Mr. Ace," he said, and the others laughed at the hilarious joke made by their leader.

Jet, so named after his brief but illustrious high school football career as a wide receiver, stepped through the obstacle course of his friends and down onto the sidewalk. His career lasted one and a half seasons.

"Follow me."

Ace noticed the two teens that were pestering him had scattered.

"Where we going?" Ace asked, still fighting to cover his nervousness.

"Right here. Welcome to my office."

Jet turned down into a small alleyway between two buildings. It was barely a pedestrian path and was littered with bottles, cans and other garbage. It also reeked of marijuana and urine.

Jet turned to face Ace.

"You got the money, honey?"

"I do, though I gotta say "$200 is a lot of money."

"What do you know about the price of a piece, man? This is a beauty, a 38 Special literally taken off a cop last month. Works like a charm - and here, a package of ammo just for you. Dude, $200 is a steal."

Jet stared at him, squinting from the smoke of a cigarette hanging out of the left corner of his mouth and going directly into his eye.

Ace was pretty sure he could not trust this street-wise goateed thug as far as he could throw him. But he also knew he wanted the gun. Anger at everything in his life at the moment was calling for revenge against the two guys that shot his father not to mention the men who burned down their store. He seethed inside.

"Alright. Same time. You give me the gun. I give you the cash." Ace held out an envelope in his left hand and Jet politely turned the gun upside down and held it with the tip of his finger by the trigger guard, a big smile on his face, revealing two gold caps.

"I'm trusting you," said Ace.

"Hey my friend, you can always trust Jet."

"If it doesn't work right, and I end up dead, I'm coming after you."

Jet laughed, and Ace found himself laughing too at the comment which now made no sense to him.

Jet threw his right arm around Ace and walked him back to the stairs.

"Tell 'em Jet sent you," he said, and his cronies laughed again at their leader.

Ace nodded and waved and felt even more confident as he made his way back through the street. Those standing around on the corners who had observed what went down decided to leave Ace alone as he strutted his way back out through the gauntlet.

Sam spun his chair around and looked over the city. Things were quiet *but it's early*.

He listened as the first ring rang out in his ear and then another. His cousin Elias lived in Montreal, Canada. He hoped he wasn't calling too early.

"Bonjour, allo?"

"Hey Cuz," Sam said jokingly. And then impersonating a mafia mobster from the streets of New York, he added, "How you doin?"

"Sam, is that you?"

"Ya man, I hope I'm not calling too early."

"Not at all. I'm up and at 'em... you know me, an early riser from way back."

The two exchanged long-time-no-talk banter for a bit and then Sam cut to the chase.

"I'm wondering if you might give me your thoughts on something... Sandra and I are looking at our options for maybe coming up your way?

"What? Really? I mean that would be awesome, like for a couple of weeks or something around Christmas maybe? You could stay here; we'd have a big reunion for sure."

"That would be fun," said Sam. "But we're thinking about something a little more permanent maybe. We just have to start somewhere."

"Seriously whoa! How cool is that?"

"Well, on one hand not so much. It is getting really weird around here, Elias. I mean, people - and by that I mean Jews - are getting jumped in broad daylight, their places burned down; protest mobs are full of hate and violence and it keeps getting worse. We're looking at getting out, you know? And I just thought I would give you a call…"

"By all means, bro. Come up. You can hang out with us until you get sorted out. I guess you have to go through Immigration and all that if you want to stay in Canada for the rest of your natural lives but hey, you can camp here."

"Thanks, man. I'm not sure what the process is, or what will happen. I'll be looking into that this week, but it's good to know there's somewhere to land."

"Hey man, always, you're family. It's gotten worse up here too, no question - as far as the antisemitic thing goes - but it doesn't sound half as bad as in your neck of the woods. There's a large Jewish community in Montreal. Just keep me informed. I'll talk to Becca." Then in his best British accent he added," Your room shall be ready, good sir."

Sam laughed and assured him they wouldn't be arriving tomorrow.

"Thanks, man, I appreciate it," he added.

"No problem. Great to hear your voice."

The two chatted a bit more before saying their goodbyes, and Sam spun his chair back around, giving himself a nod of approval just for making that call. *Sandra will be pleased.*

He got up from his desk and headed downstairs to the main part of the precinct. Devon Fletcher walked out of the lunchroom and into the same open area. The two eyed each other for a moment like two gunfighters in a Spaghetti Western movie.

Just then the captain came into the room from outside.

"Morning men!" Captain Conner said with earned authority.

The two gave their good greetings.

Then Sam saw his opportunity in front of the captain.

"Hey Devon, did you guys ever nail the killer in the Tennyson case?" He knew they hadn't.

With a feigned politeness, Fletcher said, "Nope. Some street thug named Tupper is the prime but he ain't going anywhere. We haven't moved on it yet, though. More important matters."

"Oh, I'm sure the family might be thinking otherwise. I just noticed some things… mind if I sniff around a bit?"

C.C. eyed them both as the comment hung in the air.

"Go for it," said Fletcher.

"Good. Good," said Sam. And the three went their separate ways into the day.

15

Calvin Tupper, a.k.a "Tupps" on the street, was arrested the next day and was sitting in cells desperately needing a fix.

A hardcore heroin addict for the last six years, Tupps was known by police for his petty theft - steal and sell, get a fix, steal and sell, repeat. Murder was not his gig.

He sat on the metal bed, visibly agitated in his new little gray ten-by-ten bunker, nervously bouncing his knees at a rapid pace up and down through his ripped jeans. Sam pressed him from outside the bars.

"What made you murder Mr. Tennyson, Tupps? Why did you cross the line and stab the guy so many times? What got into you? You've never done anything like that before. Look at me, Tupps, what was in your head?"

Tupps squirmed on his bed and muttered "I don't know" but Sam pressed on.

"You know that First Degree Murder gets you life in the State Penn, don't you? You realize you'll never get out. You'll have a nice little room like this for the rest of your life and…"

Tupps turned to the wall and curled up in a fetal position.

"We can make all that go away, though," said Sam.

Tupps rolled over and looked at Sam like a barnyard dog that was beaten every day with a 2X4.

"Just tell me who put you up to this Tupps. How much did they pay you? Give me a name or something I can go on, and life in long-term prison could go away. You still killed the guy but the sentence will be reduced big time if you cooperate with us."

"I... I don't know."

Sam knew Tupps was cracking and started pacing back and forth to add to the tension.

"What don't you know, Tupps? You don't know if I'm telling you the truth? I am. Or you don't know if you should tell me the truth? You should. Do the right thing, Tupps. Or maybe you don't know a name. Is that it?"

"I don't have a full name," Tupps said, shivering. "Can I get a cup of coffee maybe? I'm freezing, man."

"Sure, Tupps. Coming right up. Not a full name? That's ok, Tupps. How about half a name, a first name, a nickname, a last name... something. Who paid you?"

Tupps squeezed out a name. "Guy named Boone."

"Boone?"

"That's all I know, man! A guy named Boone contacted me and said he'd drop 2K into my lap if I did Tennyson in and made it look like a robbery. I got half before just for sayin' I'd do it… the other half came later."

"Boone," said Sam wracking his brain. "Boone."

"So you got the money?" Sam asked, trying to keep him talking. "How did you get the money?"

"I don't know, man. Some dude threw it at me from a car window; it was a foreign jobby like a Jetta or something. Merc maybe. High end. Stood out cuz it didn't belong in my neighbourhood."

"That's helpful, Tupps, very helpful. Anything else? How did you get the apartment number?"

"Nah. Nothing. I don't know nothing else. The apartment number was in a note wrapped around the money. How about that coffee?"

"Ya, ya, I'm on it right now." Sam turned to fulfill his promise and Tupps yelled after him, "Three sugars!"

"Hey, Silverman!"

The voice from a side interrogation room was Fletcher's. Sam stopped and turned toward it.

"So, any big news from our boy in there? Or did he just confess again that he was dope hungry and needed the money and yada, yada, yada, things happen?"

"Actually, there's much more to the story, but I won't bore you with the details," said Sam.

"What are you talking about?" Fletcher demanded.

"Sorry," said Sam. "I'm on a bit of a tight timeline here, got to get some jo for... for our boy there." Sam kept walking and didn't look back.

David Cain put the phone down. His father was dead. Cain breathed deeply through his nose.

"Well, that's that," he said out loud to no one. He loathed the idea of going back to Armarillo and going through the motions of a big family funeral. *I may just have to be out of the country.*

He pushed the intercom's red button and Sonia Tally responded by gliding through the door.

"You rang, Master?" She said with a smile.

Cain laughed and was reminded of the TV sitcom *I Dream of Jeannie*, where actress

Barbara Eden would call her boss, played by
Larry Hagman, "Master."

"I like that… Master. Has a nice ring to it.
Sonia, would you set up a flight to Amarillo for
sometime next week? My father kicked the
bucket and I gotta go back there, you know, for
appearance's sake."

"Oh, I'm sorry."

"What are you sorry for? Just charter the
plane."

"Of course," she said, feeling a little
dismissed. "Anything else, your majesty."

Cain looked up at her. He was more than a
little tired of her ways but tolerated her on
account of his need for pretty things around
him at certain times.

"I'm sorry, I didn't mean to be rude. I'm, you
know, grieving, dealing with his death and all."

Sonia squinted at him, knowing better, but
tolerated his behaviour on account of her need
for his money and the high life of New York
City.

"By the way, everything's set for tomorrow
night. I assumed you'd like me there," she said.

"Of course," he said. "Dressed in your
gorgeous best, if you please. It's going to be a
great night."

Tomorrow night was more important in
Cain's mind than a weekend family funeral in

Amarillo. The gala fundraising event for his human rights charity work through PVI would draw millionaires and other tycoon-wannabes. They would be flooding the Cipriani 42nd Street ballroom, one of Manhattan's top ballrooms for a dinner and art auction. The room's 1920s decor, pillars and high ceilings make it appear like the set of *The Great Gatsby,* one of Cain's favourite movies, and it was the perfect setting for a grand art sale. Opulence and decadence would be the order of the day.

Across the city, FBI Special Agent Frank Hanover was doing his utmost to obtain two tickets to Cain's PVI Dinner & Auction for when the doors opened.

"Sir, we need to get in there to get an audience with Cain," Hanover said into his phone. "Tickets are going fast."

"But it's $5,000 a pop for dinner and what… a conversation? A conversation that isn't even certain?" Deputy Director Douglas DeAngelos muttered a curse at his special agent. "I can't see it, Frank."

"Sir, we have reason to believe this guy virtually pulled the trigger in an assassination attempt on our president, not to mention a series of other hate crimes that I'm piecing together. I think if I can talk with him directly, and he takes the bait we're offering, he will open up to me. I know how he thinks… I just need this one opportunity."

There was a long silence on the other end of the line.

"And it's for charity," added Frank with a hopeful twist.

"I'll see what I can do." CLICK.

Frank hung up his phone and looked at Davis.

"I think we need to pick up some tuxedos boyo! We're going to the ball."

16

Sam rapped on the wooden part of the screen door and noticed a couple of chips of white paint fly off in escape.

Maria Davidson opened the inner door and didn't conceal her delight in seeing Sam.

"Officer Silverman! What a delight! Come on in!" She pushed the screen door in Sam's direction and he deftly stepped aside.

"Please, call me Sam," he said.

Maria offered Sam a coffee and he received it with gladness. It was chilly out and snow was beginning to fall.

Sam followed her into the living room where Zach was dressed in regular clothes and sitting in his recliner. He stood up when Sam entered the room.

"Oh, please," said Sam waving off any formalities. "Just came to see how you guys are doing."

"Thank you very much," said Zach, sitting back down and pointing Sam to the adjacent recliner.

Their daughter Shelly was sitting on a spot at a small table, working on a puzzle and Ace sat cross-legged on the floor following a sports report on television about the Minnesota Timberwolves' good start to their season.

"How's the recovery going, Zach?" Sam asked as he took the coffee from Maria's hands. "Thank you."

"Going pretty good. I'd say I'm ready to go back to work, but of course, there's no work for me to go back to."

"Any word on the fire investigation?"

Zach furrowed his brow. "I doubt they'll ever catch those upstanding citizens. And I get the feeling the cops aren't really doing their utmost to find them either. No offense."

Sam nodded. "None taken," he said.

"Meanwhile, our insurance is in process. But I'm not even sure I want to go back again to the whole supermarket world. I'm a little gun-shy if you know what I mean."

"Of course. If there's anything Sandra and I can do…"

"We're doing good but thanks, Sam. It means a lot."

Ace got up and went into the kitchen area and Sam remembered seeing him on the street corner a while back.

Sam wanted to talk to him about that but wasn't sure how to crack open that conversation.

"I'm going to go shoot some hoops at the school," Ace said, re-entering the threshold.

"Are you sure?" Zach asked. "It's pretty cold out there."

"Ya, I'm dressed for it. I'll be back by 6."

"Be safe and be aware, son. There's a lot of hate in our neighbourhood."

"Oh I am, Dad, don't worry," said Ace and then was gone before his father could change his mind.

Sam stood up and took another sip of his coffee.

"There really is a lot of stuff happening out there, Zach. Make sure he's being safe, eh."

"I cannot believe what's going on," said Zach. "Ever since the U.S. backed off in their support of Israel, all hell has been breaking loose."

"Well, we need to stick together, you know?" Sam looked at Zach as if he was peeking over his glasses, except he wasn't wearing glasses.

~

A half-hour later Sam turned out of the alley beside the Davidson house toward the high school and breathed out loud, "Just as I thought."

Ace wasn't shooting hoops. It may have been some of his team he was with but they were sitting on a concrete picnic bench at the high school. A couple of them were vaping. One did have a basketball in his hands.

Sam pulled over and stood up out of the driver's door with one foot on the ground, one in the car.

"Hey, Ace!"

The boys looked up from their phones and convos.

"Ace, can I have a word?"

Ace slipped off the table, hoodie pulled up over his head and he walked to Sam with a particular swagger that Sam recognized as "gangsta style."

"Ace, what's going on?"

"Whaddya mean?" Ace said, looking as innocent as could be.

"You seem to be… drifting, you know, from star athlete to… well, you act like you're looking for trouble."

"What kind of trouble?" Ace asked.

"You tell me. What kind of trouble are you looking for, Ace? The revenge kind?"

"Maybe I am, maybe I ain't."

"Listen I've seen this before, bro. Even if you ever see those punks again and you go after them, the repercussions of hammering them, or worse, would be far greater than what you could do to them."

Ace just stared at the ground.

"I'm serious, Ace. You do them in, and you're the one that breaks your parents' hearts. They don't need you going off and getting into trouble now, and ending up in jail, do they?"

Ace looked at Sam in the eyes for a second.

"Do they, Ace?"

"No."

"Listen, you let us nail those guys. We'll do far more to punish them than you can." And then he added, "Listen, if you ever need to chat, here's my number." Sam gave Ace his card, which he promptly tucked into his hoodie and walked away, sauntering back to the picnic table.

Elias and Becca Campbell were in Ottawa on a bit of a weekend away, taking in an art & wine festival, touring through Parliament, and visiting a museum. They had just crossed over the Rideau Canal and were approaching

Parliament Hill on Wellington Street, warmed by the four gothic buildings standing proudly on the snow-dusted hill, namely the West Block, the Centre Block, the East Block and the Library.

Becca read from a tourist brochure: "Built in the 1859-1865 timeframe, the buildings served the united provinces of Upper and Lower Canada, and have been constantly occupied by the House of Commons, Senate and departmental offices of the new Dominion of Canada after Confederation since 1867."

"Cool," said Elias as they gazed at the buildings and looked for a parking place. Their stares were broken by about 150 anti-Israel protesters outside of the Centre Block, directly across from the Israeli Embassy on O'Connor Street, waving flags and banners and chanting for Israel to be destroyed. Hundreds of them were making their way down from O'Connor Street toward the Hill. They were wearing masks to hide their identities.

Elias put on the brakes and paused for a moment.

"What are you doing?" Becca asked.

"Thinking. Do we risk walking through this mob just to see some old buildings?"

"Well, I'm asking you what are you doing, meaning what are you waiting for? Let's get out of here!"

Elias looked in his rearview mirror and despite traffic beginning to line up behind him, did a three-point turn and drove away from the protest, back toward Rideau. He had read enough and seen enough on the Internet and on television that told him it would be unwise to stick around.

"So much for our little adventure," he said. "These are the same players we see in Montreal all the time - same signs, same get-ups. Freakin' gong show! Afraid to show their faces. They have no idea what they're talking about. They chant 'from the river to the sea' but they don't even know what river or what sea they're yelling about."

Elias went on for about 20 minutes about how the West is being won over by Hamas and others of the same mind, and how Israel has been losing favour globally, despite being the only democracy in the Middle East.

"People are calling white black and black white, good bad and evil good, darkness light and light darkness," he concluded, quoting a passage from the Old Testament.

"When they scream their protests about Israel, they have no idea that they are the ones calling for genocide! They are pulling directly from the Hamas charter. They think it will be some sort of Eutopia where Israel will be no more and Palestinians will run the show, and the Jews will be happy to live there. They forget that Christians and Jews have been totally eradicated from most countries in the Middle East. The only democracy in the Middle East that allows Christians, even Jewish believers like us, is in fact, Israel!"

Becca reached across the console and grabbed his hand to calm him down.

"Drives me nuts!" he said. "And, it's getting worse every day. A Jew can't even wear a fedora these days. I mean, the Arab world does not save, protect, or help the Jews. They want to do away with them. It's in their charters."

"I know, I know. You're getting worked up honey, and you need to watch your blood pressure," Becca said. "Let's just get out of here and find a coffee shop or a bakery we can sit for a while."

17

All the magnates and moguls were dressed in their best at the Cipriani 42nd Street ballroom, each either with a wine glass in one hand and a pretty lady on the other or they were also pretty ladies reversing the roles who had a young man hanging on their arm or trailing behind them like a puppy dog. They wandered through the opulence and resplendence of the grand hall, viewing each exhibit and comparing the notes in their program with the real deal as if they were experts in historical art. Few were.

Most of the exhibits dated between the late 1800s and 1940's with much adieu given to the paintings and statues of Nazi Germany. Each ticket holder was given a fancy baton to hold for when the auction commenced. Anticipation was high and filtered through the classical music being piped in the overhead speakers. Servers moved in and out of the crowd offering top-ups on champagne and delicate finger foods.

Frank Hanover and Andrew Davis, both dressed in black tuxes, white dress shirts with matching black bowties, sauntered through the gallery, pretending to know the pieces like the rest of them, inching ever closer to David Cain. Frank was conspicuously handcuffed to a briefcase and would stop at various paintings in the Nazi Germany section, stroking his chin pensively and mentally calculating.

"Enjoying the show?"

Frank was waiting for this.

"Ah, immensely," said Frank looking back and forth between the painting they stood before and David Cain as if the painting drew his attention much more than the conversation.

"I am amazed at the collection. It is more than I… wait, aren't you David C. Cain, the curator, well not curator, forgive me, the collector if you will?"

"Yes, yes I am," said Cain, who sipped a drink from his ginger ale in a wine glass, enjoying the recognition. "I'm glad you like it."

"Oh, it is very impressive. Cheers," Frank said as he lifted his glass to clink Cain's.

"I am curious though, perhaps a little surprised about one thing."

"Oh, what's that?"

"Well," said Frank, "I see you only have two pieces from Zeigler and I believe one of those is a reproduction. It is a reproduction, isn't it? *The Four Elements* painting?"

Frank knew the 1937 work was one of Zeigler's most famous, and most reproduced as well. It depicted four naked women in allegorical poses representing both the beauty of the German race and the elements of fire, earth, water and air.

"You are quite perceptive, Mr...? I'm sorry, I didn't catch your name."

Frank smiled and said, "I didn't give it." He put his glass on a table and held out his unbound hand and said, "Marcus Alexander" in greeting.

Cain shook it with a slight upward turn of his head and said, "That sounds like a Roman Emperor's name."

"It is meant to. My father was a history professor and his specialty was Rome. He didn't want to overdo it by giving me Didius as a middle name but he still used a D-name - Marcus Denver Alexander. I was born in Denver, Colorado," Frank lied and shook Cain's hand a little more enthusiastically. "I guess he was saving me from being bullied as well," he added.

"Good to meet you, Marcus," said Cain, eyeing the briefcase just as Frank intended. "Can I call you Marcus?"

"Yes, indeed."

With a chin-nod to the briefcase, Cain said, "You came prepared… is that cash in there or gold bricks maybe?"

Frank laughed.

"No, no, just something that a real collector might be interested in."

Cain was nibbling like a brookie trout jabbing at a black fly on the business end of a fishing line.

Frank was pleased everything was going according to plan. A.J. was across the room watching his every move.

The First Presbyterian Church of Manhattan was huge. Built in the 1700s it was a complex labyrinth of gothic-style halls with massive doors and stained glass windows.

The pastor, Chauncy Andrews, whom Oliver Braxton had never met officially, was waxing eloquent from the one book of the Bible that Oliver was familiar with - the Book of Esther.

Braxton sat up and leaned in when Pastor Andrews mentioned Haman again, the homicidal villain of the ancient story, saying, "Right now Israel is fighting enemies such as Hamas and Hezbollah, but those enemies of

Israel - and civilization, I might add, are a modern-day Haman." The pastor was in a sermon series on the Book of Esther.

Oliver thought back to his conversations with Sam as they were unravelling the murder mystery of New York lawyer, Albert Yettermen, how a murderous plot dubbed H24 (H for Haman) was foiled by their efforts.

"Esther's uncle, Mordecai was calling Esther to stand up for the Jews, to stand up for Israel," Pastor Andrews said. "And, by extension he is calling us to do the same, to stand up, to be as Esther was in a sense, and to say what Esther said, "If I die, I die."

Oliver looked around and could see that some of the Friday night parishioners did not like this message. He felt for the young pastor, maybe in his late 20s, who must have been experiencing, right then and there, the intense pressure mounting against anyone who stood up for righteousness, particularly in support of Israel.

"Hamas must be destroyed, will be destroyed. God will do this in unexpected ways, just like He did back then - Haman ended up dying on a gallows made by his own hand. You'll see. Mark my words. But for us now, we must do our part and pray for the peace of Jerusalem, pray for the wisdom of the governments and authorities above us, even in our own land, and pray for those in Israel. Pray for all who mourn. Pray. Pray. Pray."

The pastor went on to say that the "days are evil" and that they point to the soon return of Jesus Christ, and he concluded his message by calling the people to stand up and join in a heartfelt prayer for Israel as well as a prayer for "courage in the times we are living in."

Oliver stood up and bowed his head, sensing many eyes on him, as not everyone stood with him. It seemed to him, though, that there were more people standing in the auditorium than were sitting. A few took the opportunity to stand up but then walked out the back door, every step reverberating in loud echoes.

As was tradition, Oliver waited in line to shake the pastor's hand as the evening wound down and to tell him what a good job he did. "Good word, Pastor," people would say. Oliver was learning.

Though it was the custom, he meant it quite seriously this night and was happy to stand in line as people milled their way out the door into the chilly winter's eve.

18

Hatred for anything Jewish was mounting in North America. Articles in prominent magazines and newspapers blamed Israel for everything from economic downturns to the federal election outcome and even climate change. Hollywood turned a corner in the summer of '24 that had arch villains on the big screens inevitably Jewish or tied to Israel in some manner.

On Monday morning Sam had turned the deadbolt in the door of his townhouse and unthinkingly made his way down the walk before he realized something was wrong.

A group of masked men and women huddled around a makeshift bonfire toward the left of his driveway where the concrete met the pavement.

He stopped and ascertained his surroundings. The masks seemed more than just winter gear. Too late to go back to the house and fiddle with his keys - Sandra was sleeping and he didn't want to endanger her.

The mob stared at him and a few of them started moving toward him. Before he had a chance to draw his revolver, they rushed him. They had batons and sticks and who knows what other weapons. Sam reacted instinctively and met the first man squarely with a right cross into the invader's jaw, falling him instantly into the path of the others. Sam cut to his left and ran through the next one, which happened to be a woman who flew about four feet in the air, landing hard. He continued to run somewhat awkwardly in the freshly fallen snow to the little three-foot fence that separated his home from his neighbour's. He cleared that easily and kept running as the mob doing their best to keep up with him. They were out for blood, and Sam was out for survival. Fear and adrenalin took over his entire body. On the sidewalk, he turned a corner down a gravelled alley with the masked mob about 20 or 30 yards behind.

"In here, Sam! Quick."

The voice came as a surprise to Sam but he recognized it as the homeless man he befriended outside the hospital weeks ago. Sam looked toward the sound of the voice, and there was Allan, gesturing Sam with a fingerless glove toward a makeshift doorway through wooden pallets, garbage and an old recliner.

Sam stopped and then flew to the doorway, which Allan quickly covered back up with the pallets.

"It's one of my favourite spots for sleeping," he said with a grin. "Now, quiet your breathing, pardner."

The mob raced by the hiding spot with Allan and Sam peering at them through the shadows of the pallets in the morning sun.

Sam counted nine chasers and was thankful that he led them away from his home. *But why were they posted at my property in the first place?*

He was visibly shaken, even trembling inside but police instincts steadied his nerves. In a lowered whisper, he thanked Allan for rescuing him.

"Well, I said I owed you one," Allan said with his toothless grin.

Sam eased his way past the pallets and back out into the alley. He jogged back to the house, double-checking the deadbolt. He got into his car and breathed deeply. He began rethinking his reactions and wished he had pulled his gun but was glad he got one good crack in before fleeing into the alley. He was also thankful that none of the thugs had the good sense to follow where his tracks led in the mud and snow. He made a mental note to thank Allan in a more meaningful way.

As he drove toward the precinct, he noticed several more bonfires with groups of people warming themselves. *What is this place coming to?* Most wore balaclavas or ski masks that could be pulled down over their faces at a moment's notice. They leered at him as he drove by slowly. He glanced at the time on the dashboard, 7:33 a.m. A growing sense of doom rippled its way through his body.

More and more, Sam was becoming certain it was time to get out of the States.

The sun was just beginning to dip into the Gulf of Thailand where Lester Boone drifted in and out of sleep, soaking up the last rays of the day at Ko Samet Beach, not far from his favourite hotel, the Hilton Pattaya.

For someone normally quite adept at evade & escape maneuvers, Lester had become far too complacent in Thailand, even for his own liking. He did not pick up on the fact that several FBI agents temporarily working with Interpol and local law enforcement had surrounded him, on lounge chairs under big umbrellas, walking along the beach in pairs, and even selling ice cream from a little peddle-operated bicycle with two coolers strapped on either side. They were moving closer to him every 30 seconds or so. If he had been paying attention, he would've noticed more than one touching their ear in a conversation.

19

As Frank had explained it to DeAngelos, he had introduced to Cain at the ballroom A.J. Davis as his business partner, Todd Adams, and Cain shook his hand with some enthusiasm.

"So, Marcus, what do you have in there that is so interesting?" Cain asked with a nod to the briefcase.

"I'd rather not say it out here. Do you have somewhere where we could meet in private? I'll show you," Frank responded.

"Sure, Marcus, sure," said Cain, and added to them both, "Follow me," and they did across the ballroom to a mirrored door that led into a back room.

The room was not as opulent as the main hall but was still impressive with a 1920's decor. A couch, a chair and a loveseat had the fireplace surrounded and a small bar was off to one side. Cain gestured for the men to take a seat on the couch while he walked to the bar.

"Do you want anything?" he asked of his new-found friends.

"No thanks," they said almost too simultaneously and thought the better of it.

Frank asked A.J. for the key to the cuffs and Cain smiled at how they were being so secure with whatever was in there.

A few clicks and pops later, Frank produced the Zeigler sketches.

Cain put his ginger ale on the bar and strained to hide his delight. Frank was pleased as he took the bait.

"Are these…?"

"Yes they are," said Frank. "These are original paint sketches and pencil drawings of Adolf Zeigler for his famous *Judgement of Paris* painting."

Cain was awed with wonder and asked if he could touch it.

"Just at the edges, if you please," said Frank.

"Of course, of course," said Cain and he lifted the piece to the light. "This is impossible. No one has ever produced… I've never seen."

"Well, you're quite right, sir. No one has ever seen these, not in our day anyway, because they were locked up in the vault of one sir Richard Ellington of London, England, along with this," Frank said holding up a reproduction of another famous Nazi prize. "And some of his own works, too, of course, but I doubt you'd be interested in those."

"Yes, yes," said Cain quite distracted by the Zeigler sketches. "He is my favourite artist, you know."

"Ah," said Frank. "Mine too - well and Hitler's as well."

"I think you and I will become very good friends, Mr. Alexander," said Cain, as he peered at the fake Zeigler.

Frank glanced at A.J. with a knowing look, which A.J. quickly acknowledged with a nod like the nod you'd get when someone you just passed a basketball to, scored a bucket.

Everything was going perfectly that night.

As Sandra Silverman rolled the garbage bin to the curb, she saw the remains of a fire at the edge of their driveway and a blood spot on their sidewalk. She looked up and down the streets but they were empty, other than Mrs. Batterson rolling her bin to the curb as well. She waved. Mrs. Batterson gave her usual wave back. Sandra pulled her cell phone out as she walked back to the house.

"Hey Darlin," Sam said. "How are you this fine morning?"

"Well, I'm wondering if you had a little campfire this morning at the end of the drive…"

Sam was hoping against hope that she would've missed that little burn, but he knew better. He was anticipating the call.

"Ya, there was a little incident this morning."

"A little incident? Like what?" She was feisty this morning, tired of all the violence and disrespect that was happening in their neighbourhood.

"Ya, I was sort of chased down the back alley."

"What? What are you talking about? Are you okay? Was anybody hurt? There's blood on the sidewalk! What happened? Where are you now?"

"Hey, one question at a time," he tried to sound jovial. "I'm alright, all good; I'm at the precinct. Everything's fine. Just some rowdies. I did get a shot in."

"A shot? You pulled your gun?"

"No, no, I mean a shot as in punch. I knocked a guy flat on his keister. You would've been proud of me, honey. But ya, everything's fine. They're gone. No real harm done."

She knew Sam was trying to minimize a very serious situation.

"Sam, don't patronize me. Are you saying you were chased by some KKK group or something? What are you saying?" She demanded an answer.

"Well, it was a group of anti-Israel rowdies, yes, but I split down the alley - and you know that homeless dude from a while back? Allan? He actually rescued me by ducking me into his little hovel. The group totally ran on by and I never saw them again."

There was a moment of silence on the phone and Sam realized he heard Sandra sniff.

"Hey, are you crying, Sand? It's okay. Really, it is."

"I don't feel okay, Sam. I don't feel okay. Everywhere I turn, everywhere I look, things keep happening and it just keeps getting worse."

"I know. I know. I'm working on it."

"Really, Sam? Are you? Cuz I'm done here." And then she repeated herself for emphasis. "I'm done."

By the time Sam hung up the phone, Sandra had settled down a fair bit but was still fearfully looking out the windows as she spoke to him.

He took her, "I'm done" comment very seriously, and knew he needed to come up with a plan to get to Canada, maybe even to Israel if need be. *And probably sooner than later.*

He would call his cousin that afternoon and start the process with Immigration Canada as well.

He was sitting at his desk and looking again at the Tennyson file when C.C. knocked and popped his head in the door.

"Hey Cap," said Sam.

"Sam, what's the status on the Tennyson case? Are you pressing any further with this Tupps guy?"

"Well, he will definitely do some time for manslaughter at least but he gave us a name that I'm pursuing, a guy named Boone."

"Who's he?"

"There's more than a few Boones in the phonebook, sir," said Sam, "but we've narrowed it down to about 10 Boones who have records, none with the kind of record that would indicate murder, though and about five with connections to organized crime. One guy has some interesting connections that I'm still looking into."

"Ok. Keep me posted. For some reason, the higher-ups are interested," C.C. said.

"Will do," said Sam. *Why are they interested?*

"Inquiring minds want to know," said Sam jokingly.

20

Deputy Director Douglas DeAngelos enjoyed the full report verbally. But also wanted a digital report from Frank by morning. After all, he had wrangled $10,000 for the tickets.

"I hope your dinner was worth the big bucks," he said.

"Well, you'll be happy to know that it was a fine meal, sir, steak and lobster with all the fixings. For dessert, I had a Tonka Bean Panna Cotta, Poached Raspberries, Raspberry Foam, and Buckwheat Ice Cream over a bed of roasted walnuts. I'm not sure what Agent Davis had. Just a second…"

"That's enough, Frank. Just get on with it. So, what happened with Cain after that?

Frank held back a bit of a chuckle, as he could have given more food details, not to mention the auction.

"You'll also be happy to know that we didn't purchase any art," said Frank.

"Thank God for that," said DeAngelos.

"Well, Cain bit for sure," said Frank. He liked the Zeigler sketches and wants to negotiate a price. We never got down to brass tacks money-wise. But I'm sure he believed my story about me being a Hitler fan and he opened up about some of his efforts below the surface of his PVI charity - I definitely need more of his time. He had to disengage for the auction, but he indicated that he has a large following of people who are on the same page about the Jewish Two-State problem, which is just a reshuffling of the cards from the *"Jewish problem"* of the 1930s. I said my underlying motivation in life was to find a *solution if you know what I mean*, and he knew exactly what I meant. In fact, he just ate it up. So, all in all, it went very well. We have another meeting on Wednesday to talk price and gain more insight."

"Good work, Frank. Be careful - this guy has a lot more going on than even we know about in the so-called dark web out there," DeAngelos added. "He could turn on you in a second."

"You bet. I think the art was the perfect bait for Cain. Next time one of us will wear a wire and see if we can't pull more info out about the whole presidential assassination conspiracy."

Lester Boone didn't know what hit him. One moment he was enjoying a margarita on a sunset beach and the next moment he was swarmed by what he thought were 30 or 40 FBI agents. In reality, it was a few local law enforcement officers working undercover with

Interpol and the FBI, which has limited authority outside the United States. The FBI must always work with local police and are not even allowed to carry weapons or make arrests in other countries without governmental permission.

Boone never stopped declaring his innocence of any crime, but he still ended up in lockup awaiting charges of conspiracy to commit murder. The international agents knew they couldn't pin anything on him, but they wanted to tenderize him a little to see if he would spill a name or two behind the assassination attempt of last April.

FBI agent Malcolm Webster, a 22-year veteran committed to the tightly cropped crewcut of the '50s though due to the hotter climate, had given up the grey suit for khakis and a polo shirt. He led the interview.

Webb, as he was known, grew up in St. Petersburg, Mississippi and his slow drawl reflected his heritage.

"Lester, we know you were in D.C. at the time of the shooting. Few people could make a shot like that, very few, but we can't seem to find a motivation for you… other than money, I suppose."

He continued. "April 24… Do you remember where you were, Lester, and what you were up to on April 24? Can anyone vouch for your whereabouts on that day? Did someone pay you to make that shot? How much would it have taken for you to do the deed? Or did you just work on your own because you have some sort of problem with Madam President? Maybe you were just in a bad mood that day, maybe woke up on the wrong side of the bed? Just stirring up stuff? Did you mean to hit her in the shoulder? I think that you could've put that slug in her eye if you wanted to, don't you? If you ask me, I'm a bit surprised, given your expertise, that you would lower your standards to just hit the shoulder and then plug a few misses into the back wall. You're better than that. Or maybe you're losing it in your old age, eh? Is that it? Did you work with anybody else that day? Did someone drive for you, you know, a getaway vehicle?"

The interview lasted for an hour and a half and Lester sat silent throughout the entire process.

He was put back in cells as the team gathered to rethink their strategy.

21

It's awkward enough when two men end up at bathroom urinals at the same time, but when Devon Fletcher and Sam happen to be the men in question, awkward wasn't the word.

"Fancy meeting you here," Fletcher said. "What's the latest on Tennyson?"

"Well," said Sam. "I can't quite recall all the details at the moment. I'd have to check my notes."

"Figures. There's nothing there, Silverman. Tupps needed a fix, broke into the apartment to rob it and was met by a drunken Tennyson. The rest is history."

"What about Boone?"

Sam regretted saying Boone's name even as it slipped past his teeth.

"Who?" Fletcher finished his business and was washing his hands. "Who's Boone?"

"Probably nobody. Never mind," said Sam.

"Boone. You going after Daniel Boone now, king of the wild frontier, Silverman?" Fletcher laughed out loud at his joke as he exited the washroom, and Sam was glad to see him go.

That was so stupid, Sam. Keep your mouth shut.

Sam finished up and got back to work. He wanted to dig a bit more into the relationship between cousins Geoffrey Tennyson and David C. Cain.

Back at his desk, he took the notes Ollie had emailed him and began to read.

Geoffrey and David were born 20 months apart. Their mothers were sisters. Both grew up in Amarillo, Texas, both part of the same hardcore fundamentalist church community, snake-handling kind, though in quite different congregations across the city. It seemed David left his parents' church in his teens but Geoffrey stayed the course, even later becoming a deacon in his family's group. He was married in Amarillo, but divorced after three years and left the city in shame and disgrace.

One significant difference between these two churches the two attended that stood out to me is that one was antisemitic and the other was pro-Israel. You can guess which was which. Weird though, because they're in the same denomination but I guess that's pretty common cuz it's more of a fellowship than a denomination; each church is autonomous and depending on the pastor and the leaders, can bounce in all sorts of directions. Anyway, Geoffrey grew up loving Israel; David did not. David ended up rebelling against his parents'

*church anyway, though, so I'm not sure where
it all leads. I'll keep looking.*

   Talk to ya soon,
   Ollie

   Sam leaned back in his chair and
contemplated the email, processing out loud as
was his custom.

   "What if Cain rebelled against the church
but kept his ties to antisemitism? What if he got
worse? What if Tennyson was calling it out?
What if we found some evidence of that? Is
there an email or something, pointing to Cain
in any way? That would be good but where do
we look that we haven't already looked? We
might not have picked up on an email to Cain
before…"

   He gave a slight wave to his secretary
through the glass door as she looked up from
her desk at the sound of his voice. She went
back to her work.

   He decided to go down to EVIDENCE to see
if there was anything he missed, a file folder, a
letter, an email, or some pointer that wasn't
picked up in the first go-round.

   Ace ran his fingers over the handle of the
revolver in his hoodie while eyeing the group of
guys in front of the Third Street Candy Store.

He was 99 percent sure one of them was the same Neanderthal who pulled the trigger the night his father Zach was shot and his own teenage life was turned upside down.

He felt the hair on the back of his neck stand to attention as a rush of heat raced from the bottom of his feet to the top of his head. Adrenalin was pumping throughout his body. He was familiar with that feeling but not with the circumstances or reasons why this time.

He moved closer for a better look and more importantly to try to hear the guy's voice.

The man was wearing black sweatpants just like that night. He had a fake leather jacket on and topped his ensemble with a black toque and gloves. He held some dice in his right hand and rolled them incessantly around and against each other in his palm as if he was about to roll them. But he never did.

Ace was less than six feet away when he was noticed by one of the guys.

"Hey man, whatta you want?"

Others turned and looked in Ace's direction, who wrapped his fingers around the handle and trigger of the '38 Special hidden within the hoodie.

The guy took a long drag on a cigarette and blew it at Ace.

"I asked you a question, jock."

Though he could've shot straight through his hoodie, Ace suddenly pulled the gun out and some of the cronies scattered immediately, including the one asking the questions. Ace pointed his weapon directly at his target.

"Whoa, dude, easy…that ain't no toy. You got a problem?"

His name was Billy Grandler. He was known as 'Wild Bill.'

"Ya, I do. It's you. You're my problem and this is the cure," Ace said it as he twisted the gun. He realized the words that came out of his mouth sounded way cornier than they had when he was practicing in his mirror back home.

"You just confirmed for me who you are. I'll never forget your voice, man."

"Who are you, dude? I don't know you," said Wild Bill nervously.

Remember that guy you shot at Zach's Store robbery? That was my father, man!"

"Hey, that was an accident, man," Wild Bill claimed while raising his hands and holding their palms out toward Ace.

Just then the door to the candy store burst opened with a ringing of a bell, and Monty Brown, the grizzled but kindly old shopkeeper, stepped out wielding a four-foot lead pipe.

"What's going on here? You kids need to get outta here before I knock you out. This is my place!" He waved the pipe above his head. "I'm serious! Now would be a good time to scram!"

As Ace glanced toward the doorway and the overweight Monty looming larger with his lead pipe by the second, Wild Bill took the opportunity to charge at Ace, hitting him squarely in the chest.

The fiery blast of Ace's '38 cracked the sounds of the street with a piercing echo and the unmistakable smell of gunpowder and metal wafted in the air as Ace and Wild Bill went down to the concrete together.

22

It was an outdoor market on Hudson Street overlooking the Hudson River that Cain chose as a meeting place. A little bistro, called *Pat's Place* specializing in fancy coffees and pastries was the spot of his choosing.

Frank and A.J. sat sipping their drinks and A.J. had what he described as the best bagel ever.

A.J. was wearing a wire taped to his chest while a white van, known as a 'quaker van', marked as Johnson & Bailey's Bakery was parked half a block away recording their every word. Two other agents, Jan Fencer and Kennedy Allyn, sat at a nearby table sipping lattes and ready for come what may.

Frank suddenly stood up and welcomed Cain as he approached from behind A.J.

"Good morning!" Frank said enthusiastically. "How are you this fine New York day?"

Cain was just as jovial and said, "Great Marcus, how are you?" He greeted A.J., whom he knew as Todd, with the same enthusiasm.

Before Frank could answer, Cain announced, "I'm just going to grab a coffee," and then moved to the counter, adding, "This place is one of my favourite hidden gems."

What happened next could have been the worst mistake in the career of A.J. Davis. He touched his ear and said, "Copy that?"

"Copy," the techs in the bakery van responded accordingly.

But it was Frank's remonstrating glare at Davis that was picked up by Cain, whose self-protective radar suddenly went off inside him. He was immediately suspicious though he didn't know why.

Cain paid for his $6 Americano with a $10 bill and said, "Keep it" to the lady behind the counter.

He turned and faced the two agents and walked pensively toward them.

"So," said Cain politely. "Tell me again how you came into possession of the Zeigler sketches."

Frank gave much detail about how they were in a vault below the estate of Sir Richard Ellington, a former banker in the 1950s-60s. He retired in 1970 and spent much of his later years as a recluse, estranged from his ex-wife, son and daughter, eventually dying in 1988 with most of his wealth being left to the Historic England Foundation. His son and daughter kept the title and lands but any money he had in accounts went to the government.

"The son & daughter, I believe, contested the will, but to no avail. So, as sort of a just-to-spite-Dad sale, they sold off most of the possessions in the house, and that's how I came across it."

"Do tell," said Cain.

"I just happened to be in London visiting my wife's family, when I noticed an estate sale ad in a local paper," said Frank. "I can't recall what paper… doesn't matter I suppose. I took it as a bit of an escape from the family stuff, if you know what I mean, to take a drive out of the city and well, you never know what you may find in one of those estate sales, especially over there…some of the estates are amazing themselves, and… "

Cain lifted his hand to stop the run-on sentence. Frank was grateful.
"So you purchased it at a glorified boot sale as well as another historical painting and you want how much for it now?" Cain was cutting right to the chase.

"From my research, Zeiglar's work goes anywhere from $127,000 to $1.5 depending on, well, depending on many things," said Frank.

"True," said Cain. "But those numbers are for finished pieces, of course. Those sketches you have are just that, sketches. They're incomplete."

"All the more authentic, and rare," said Frank. "Did you know he was Hitler's favourite artist?"

"Yes, I did," said Cain. "So, what we are talking about here, Marcus?"

"Are you a fan? I understood you were from our conversation the other night," said Frank, baiting Cain a little deeper.

"Oh, quite. I am. May I see the sketches again?"

"Of course," said Frank. "Todd, will you show him the sketches again?"

"You bet," said A.J. and proceeded to unlock the briefcase.

He gently pulled out the pieces, leaving the other painting inside its tube in the briefcase.

Cain painstakingly took the historical beauty from A.J. and said with a smile, "I could just take it and run, now, couldn't I?"

"I'm glad you said that with a grin," said Frank. "I'm fast but Todd here was an all-state linebacker back in the day."

Cain looked at Frank wryly but never gave A.J. another glace.

"It is very beautiful." Cain took out a small magnifying lens and held it to his right eye and peered at the sketches.

"I would love to study it some more before I make an official offer, but I'm thinking of something in the neighbourhood of $200,000."

Frank didn't change his screensaver face but nodded his acknowledgement and took the drawings from Cain, and gave them to A.J. who gently rolled them and tucked them into the case.

"Changing the subject a little bit," said Frank, "do you remember that fella that got charged with the assassination attempt of the president back in the spring sometime?"

"I do. Why do you ask?"

"Well, apparently he got off scot-free but was taken out by a fellow fan if you know what I mean."

"Hmm," said Cain. "That's a shame." He took a sip of his Americano and then said, "That he got off I mean."

Frank laughed. "Indeed."

"Can you imagine," A.J. said, "how a presidential assassination by a Jew could turn the whole tide against them?"

"Can I?" said Frank, milking the topic. "They need to go back to their own country, and then that country needs to go back to its real owners."

Cain looked at his compadres and took another sip of his coffee.

"You know, I'm having a little shindig this weekend, on Saturday afternoon at my office next to the UN building, a little fundraiser for PVI, but there are a few other partners I would like you to meet… if you're interested. They are, let's say, of the same mind."

"Sounds interesting," Frank said. "Count us in."

"Bring the sketches and we can finalize a deal while we're at it," Cain added as he stood to make his exit.

Frank stood and shook his hand. A.J. did the same.

Once Cain left, Frank reprimanded his younger partner for the little ear-tapping blunder adding that he wasn't sure Cain had noticed.

23

When the dust settled and Ace struggled to get to his feet, he slowly regained a sense of what had happened.

The guy had rushed him.

The gun had gone off. He looked around. The gun was gone.

Most of the rowdies had scattered like tiny crabs when a beach rock gets flipped over by a child. Other people were now filling the gaps in the crowd.

Ace looked around. He and one other were on the ground. Wild Bill was rolling back and forth in pain, holding his right thigh. Monty Brown was on his cell phone calling 911.

Ace heard someone say, "He's bleeding out!"

Ace sat up realizing for the first time the seriousness of the situation. He began to feel nauseous. This guy, maybe a few years older than himself, could lose his life if one of those main arteries was hit. He had seen enough war shows and E.R. documentaries on television to know this.

"Look man, hang in there," he said. "An ambulance is coming."

"I don't wanna die, I don't wanna die. I don't wanna die," was all Wild Bill could get out. He looked at Ace and in a second of recognition, exclaimed, "Oh it's you! No! Don't touch me!"

Ace was pressing on the wound, his hand covered in Bill's blood.

"Look, if I don't you could die!" Ace said, forgetting his hate, his bitterness and his desire for revenge. All he wanted to do now was save Bill's life.

"I don't get it," said Bill. "You come to kill me; now you're trying to save me?"

"I don't get it either," said Ace. "Just shut up and breathe."

Distant sirens wailed in the air.

Ace was struggling to regain his equilibrium but with each breath, it got better.

The paramedics soon arrived and Ace gave way to them. One of them assessing the situation looked at Ace and said, "Way to go, kid. You probably saved his life."

Ace nodded and then looked at the ground.

I almost took it too.

Monty gave him a towel to wipe his hands of Bill's blood.

Now what?

It was close to 7 p.m. when Sam turned the deadbolt and walked into his townhouse. Soft music was playing.

He dropped his satchel at the front door closet and walked further in through the living room toward the kitchen and dining room.

Candles were on the table. Sam smiled and breathed deeply. Mediterranean spices filled his senses. *Where are you?*

Sandra was untying her apron by the stove and turned toward him.

"What's this? What's the occasion?"

"I didn't know we needed an occasion," she said with coyness. "Sit down."

Sam obeyed and Sandra danced her way around the small kitchen with the expertise of the seasoned waitress she was. She brought two dishes of her best butter chicken.

She lit the two candles.

"Hey, is it Shabbat? The woman of the house is lighting the candles. What's going on?"

"Questions, questions," said Sandra. "My detective is always asking questions."

As she lit the second candle she prayed aloud, "Thank you Hashem for our life together and your gifts of light and love. May we carry Your AHAVA love with us all the time, and give it away as much as possible. Amen."

"Amen!" said Sam as she sat down. "Ok, ok, I can't take this any longer!"

As she was about to open her mouth, shards of broken glass shattered the moment as a brick catapulted through the large bay window and careened across the living room floor.

Sandra screamed.

Sam pushed hard away from the table and in the same motion drew his gun. Sandra held her face in her hands.

Sam went to the brick, which carried a hateful note. He moved to the window, avoiding the glass as he realized that anyone who threw a brick likely wasn't carrying any other weapons. Several young men were running at the north end of the street and around the corner.

"They're gone!"

Sam looked at the glass shards on the carpet and breathed out a cuss word. He walked into the dining area and put his arms around Sandra, who screamed into his bear hug.

"It's okay. We're alright," said Sam, trying his best to comfort her. It wasn't working.

"No! No, it's not okay, Sam and we're not alright!"

He rubbed her shoulders. He could feel the icy November wind working its way through the once-warm atmosphere of their home.

"At least we don't have kids to worry about in this stupid city," Sam tried.

"That's just it Sam," Sandra said through tears. "That's what this dinner was all about."

She pushed the dishes away with such force that her wine glass flew off the table and shattered.

Sam had the look of a deer caught in headlights.

"I'm pregnant, Sam!"

24

Ace was shaking and it was more than the chill in the air.

The reality of what happened in front of the candy store, and what could have happened that day was flooding his soul. Questions filled his mind.

What happened to the gun? Where is it? Who took it? Are his prints on it? What about the prints of the guy who took it? Wouldn't that guy's prints cover his prints? Will he be charged with something — assault? Attempted murder? Can he be charged? Wasn't it self-defence? Will the cops do anything at all?

He knew that he had to settle his mind from racing. That's why he was shooting hoops at an outside court in November, in the dead of a Minnesota winter. With every shot, he would spin another possible answer to a question running through the hamster wheel in his mind. He kept coming back to the fact that in the end, nothing would be done; nothing could be proven about the gun, no one knew who had it in their possession, or how the gun went off. All would be hearsay and speculation. None of the witnesses would likely want to cooperate with the police anyway, other than maybe

Monty, but then everything happened so fast in the moment, he doubted that Monty swinging his lead pipe even saw who had the gun in the first place.

Bank.

The ball went off the backboard and into the net.

Bank.

The ball soared in a long arc, obeying Ace's tightly bent wrist on his follow-through. He repeated four bank shots in a row, then worked shots from around the key or paint as he called it, and then hit several three-pointers in a row.

Still got it.

He smiled but furrowed his brow as one lingering thought kept coming back to him from different angles.

Where did your hatred go? Where did the need for revenge go? Why did I reach out to save the same dude that shot my father?

The answer to those questions seemed a million miles away.

In the chill of the air, Ace blew on his hands, took another shot and missed. The ball rolled to the chain fence and stayed there. Ace walked toward it shoving his hands in his hoodie pocket. He felt the flimsy cardboard of a business card and pulled it out. Detective Sam Silverman.

❖

In taking his leave, Sam explained to Captain Conner that he was not quitting, just taking an extended holiday and that he had a good line on the motive for Tupps' actions — money, and also a name to follow up on. The name "Boone" was narrowed down to a couple of people but only one with a tie to Hartmann Webber who had some dealings with Tennyson's cousin, David Cain. Webber was arrested in the summer by the FBI in connection with a hate crime in New York and is currently in custody, awaiting trial.

Sam also told the captain that Tennyson had emailed his cousin back in June and again in July- no one that Sam knew of had dug that far back into his emails, nor knew of the connection with Cain. Maybe it was a long shot but it seemed Tennyson was threatening to expose his cousin's plots against Jewish communities within the United States. "And that would be grounds for a motive for murder," Sam said.

Meanwhile, Sam shoved as much of their stuff into a ten-by-ten storage locker at a place called Tall Pines Storage, packed the rest of what they could into Sandra's SUV and began the 20-hour drive to the Rainy River Border Crossing at Manitoba, still a long way from Montreal. But for him, it was moving forward and was comforting to Sandra, especially with a little one on the way.

Pastor Andrews gave a particularly emotional appeal on the first Friday night Advent service in December and Ollie found himself genuinely moved.

He found himself at the front of the Presbyterian church, at the altar, as they call it, praying for God to take over.

"All the hurts," Pastor said.

"All the hurts," Ollie repeated.

"All the pain."

"All the pain."

"God, I surrender," said the Pastor. Ollie repeated his phrasing.

"Forgive me for my selfishness, me trying to control everything."

Ollie repeated and realized he was weeping as he did.

There was a moment's pause as Pastor Andrews grabbed a tissue from the altar steps and handed it to Oliver.

"Thanks," said Ollie.

"Let's continue."

Ollie nodded.

"I give up, I give in and I give all to you, in Jesus' name, amen."

Ollie prayed it thoroughly and noticed for the first time that he could remember, he felt very "light" as he would later tell Sam.

"It was like a piano was lifted off my back," he'd say. "I'm not exactly sure what happened, Sam, but I know something did happen," he said.

Sam was happy for him, though he still wrestled with the idea of God becoming a man in Jesus Christ. He couldn't wrap his head around that.

"No need to," Ollie told him. "You're on a journey just like me. And I think the God factor will all come clear soon enough."

"Hmm," said Sam. "There's a whole lot of clarity that needs to come as far as I'm concerned."

"Well, ain't no time to start talkin' to Him like the present," Ollie said.

"Oh, I talk," Sam responded. "Maybe I talk too much; maybe I need to start listening."

25

Frank and A.J. were both impressed with the view of the New York City skyline from the paneglass windows of the offices of the People for Victims of Injustice (PVI) group.

Cain and four other men, *rather large men*, thought A.J. were in the room with them, but didn't speak much. But then neither did A.J.

"I'm so glad we could all be here altogether," said Cain. "I'm glad when history & art buffs and followers of the Fuehrer come together to raise a toast." And as he held out his glass, he said, "To all which is good and right in our eyes, and to all who see things with the same perspective!"

The men all raised their glasses and chimed in with "Hear, hear!" and "Cheers!"

Frank said, "Amen" because it seemed appropriate and clinked the glass held by A.J. and the man next to him.

"Now, to the business at hand," said Cain. "The sketches if you will," he looked toward A.J. who held the coveted briefcase.

A.J. obliged and brought the case to the desk, opened it and brought out the works of art.

"Ah," said Cain. "Beautiful. Didn't I tell you, boys? So, nicely done, so perfectly crafted." Frank was taking all this in with pleasure.

"Can we talk about the price again?" Frank said to Cain.

"But of course," Cain responded with flair. It was the flair in his voice that first triggered Frank that something was wrong.

"$200K did I say? Or was it $400? Doesn't really matter. A priceless work of art like this is well, priceless. In other words, there is no price that I would pay for it. As I'm sure you know, it is a beautiful but well-crafted forgery!"

"What? No! It cannot be!" Frank stepped back like he was having a heart attack. A.J. did his best to look stunned, which wasn't difficult because he was stunned that the forgery had been discovered.

"Yes, Marcus - if that's your real name - this is a fake. And a very good one at that. Do you know how I know? Not that it matters but just for interest's sake plus I like to inspire people with my expertise in these things from time to time."

"Yes, please inspire us," said Frank.

Cain held the sketches in his hand up to the ceiling light.

"It's the paper, Frank. This kind of stitched paper wasn't invented until the 60's well after

Adolf Ziegler died in 1959 at the ripe old age of 66. So, it could not have been his work."

Again, A.J. looked stunned and glanced at Frank who was beginning to scramble inside.

"Well, I had no idea!" Frank exclaimed. "I mean, it's near perfect! My apologies, Mr. Cain. I mean, if you still want it, I could sell it for, well say for the price of a flight back home for my friend and me - maybe $2000?"

"Are you serious, Frank? I think he's serious boys. I think Mr. Marcus here or Alexander or whatever your name is, really thinks I would want to buy this from him. No. I don't want to buy it, I'm afraid. But I will keep it. And the other work you have there in that treasure chest of yours. Mr. Klein, if you will."

The one called Klein pulled out a large gun from a shoulder holster, possibly a 44 Magnum, thought Frank. Klein moved in to take the sketches.

The other men pulled weapons and pointed them at A.J. and Frank as well.

"Please, like I said," said Frank, "We had no idea, honestly. You can have the sketches and the painting too. I don't want them. And I don't need the money. Be reasonable. We're on the same side here."

"Are we, Frank?" Cain asked. "Are we on the same side, the side that always wins, the side that loves all things Nazi, the same side that still wants to eliminate the Jews to this day?"

Both Frank and A.J. emphatically nodded and said "Yes!"

Cain walked out from behind his desk and took a sip of his drink.

"I'm not so sure, Frank," he said. "What do you think, Jimmy?"

Jimmy was the man on the left, dressed in a blue suit, shirt and tie. He had no neck in A.J.'s estimation.

"Don't know, Boss," said Jimmy.

"Burt?" Cain asked the other.

Burt, also in a suit, dressed to kill, was brandishing two long scars from each side of his mouth slashed to his ears indicating he was likely from the streets of Glasgow. His thick brogue made it for certain.

"Ah dinnae ken. Ah think they're *chories*, Boss," calling them thieves as he twisted his six-inch dagger, which in his homeland, is called a *gully*. "Ah say we slice 'em and dice 'em, toss 'em into the Abhainn."

The "Glaswegian Smile" on his face is usually done with a utility knife or box cutter late at night outside a pub and leaves one with a nasty reminder that looks like an ear-to-ear grin.

Cain walked over and peered into A.J.'s eyes. Agent Davis began to sweat profusely.

"It's your move… uh… Todd," said Cain sarcastically.

A.J. pulled his Glock M-19 and trained it on Frank.

The Galilee in Israel has a certain beauty about it regardless of the season and regardless of the weather. The early rainy season in the fall and winter and the early rains in the spring bring forth an incredible array of colours in the wildflowers blanketing the rolling hills and jagged rocks.

Adon Belitz stood on the southeastern side of the Sea of Galilee on the only spot known for the ancient story in the Bible where Jesus, or Yeshua as the Jewish people know him and his mother would've called him, drove a large herd of pigs off a cliff into the Sea.

Adon was rebuilding his guiding career after Israel demolished Hamas and the northern border had quieted down. Tourism in Israel, which was almost 53% of the national economy in 2023, took a severe nosedive in 2024 due to war and the rise of antisemitism, rebounded in the fall, and then took another hit as Iran continued to use its proxies to rain down missiles into Israel. Many inbound flights to Israel halted altogether, and most airlines were on high alert.

Tourism opened again in mid-December with Christian groups continuing to be supportive by visiting the land.

Now that the war was officially over, Israel worked at repairing political breeches, the infrastructure that was damaged and the broken relationships, internationally.

Hard questions were being asked in the Knesset, the Israeli parliament, which includes both Arab and Jewish politicians, about how the war in Gaza was handled. At the same time, efforts were being made in the south to refurbish the kibbutzim and to rebuild Gaza. The agricultural lands that were devastated by the war as people, including foreign workers, fled for their lives, were being cleaned up and re-established as fruitful agricultural lands again.

Adon, however, was more concerned with his livelihood and that of his wife, Lenora and two boys Micah, 7 and Benjamin, 4. He had moved to Israel from Canada with his parents in the early 2000s and immediately after completing his language course, he took a Professional Tour Guide course offered by the

Ministry of Tourism, specializing in English and French-speaking tours.

"It is the only place around the whole of the Sea where a cliff enters the water - exactly as found in the Gospels - around the entire Kinneret and the only place where pigs were raised in the first century; we have archeological evidence of that - as well it was a place where there are tombs, first-century tombs," he said to his enthusiastic listeners, pointing to the hillside the nine stood below overlooking the sea. "And we know, the Bible says the man who was demonized lived among tombs. Nowhere else around the Sea is there such a place."

"This is really the only location where that story, where Yeshua drove a legion of devils out of a man, a Gentile man, into a herd of pigs and those pigs could have run themselves off a cliff and into the sea. It's the only place."

That concluded his discourse to a small group of nine Canadians and three Israelis on the evidence for the Biblical story. It also concluded the day's tour, which included a boat ride across the Sea, a visit to Capernaum, a stop at Tiberias for food, and now he was giving them about 15 minutes to wander around the area and process everything.

A young Canadian couple, Michael & Sarah Shepherd and her father, Richard Baumman, were talking intently about the stop.

For Michael & Sarah, they soaked up every word. The awe factor of living in Israel was ever-increasing. They had made Aliyah only months ago, returning to the land of her fathers, living in the Galilee, and now they were returning deeper and deeper into her Hebraic roots.

Michael's cell phone buzzed. He stepped aside and answered it.

"Michael Shepherd? You don't know me. My name is Sam, Sam Silverman. I'm a detective with the Minneapolis Police Department. Can I ask you a few questions?"

~

~ END OF BOOK II ~

Rick Barker has lived in 100 Mile House, B.C. for most of his life, and has pastored Cariboo Christian Life Fellowship (CCLF) with his wife Marci for over 30 years.

Titles by Rick Barker:

Kiss the Bear

Gentile Jester in the King's Court

Atticus

Artemas

The Arrival

The Seed

Parable of the Polished Arrow

From Soul to Sole

Never Again Book I

Never Again Book II - the Bait of Cain

Manufactured by Amazon.ca
Bolton, ON

39800363R00109